Chasing Truth

Truth=Freedom, Book 2

Julie Brown

Chapter One

"911, what's your emergency?"

"Someone's in my store. He busted the glass to get in."

"Are you in your store now?"

"Yes. I don't think he knows I'm here."

"Dispatching police now. Stay on the line with me, if you can. This is the address I have for you in the Winslot Shopping Village at the corner of Eidson and Marsh Streets. What's your name, honey? Can you tell me where you are so the police know where to find you?"

"Brynleigh Tavish. I'm in a storage closet towards the back of the store. B's Books." She couldn't push any farther into the tight space, her back already up against the wall and her knees crammed against the shelving unit. Brynleigh picked up a can of spray paint off the shelf next to her and held it, nozzle pointing toward the bi-fold closet doors. It wasn't much, but if she had to fight, the aerosol should give her a little time.

"Okay, Brynleigh. Help will be there soon, just stay on the line with me."

Brynleigh breathed quietly into the phone. She

could hear someone in the outer room.   The side window on the double-paned ancient door had barely made a sound when it broke, but in the silence of the bookstore, it sounded as loud as a cannon. Peeking towards the front of the store, Brynleigh had seen a silhouette unlock the door from the inside. What could someone possibly want in this old bookstore? Brynleigh read to children in the nook on the east, but they weren't valuable 1st edition books. Normal kids books. She provided a couple of computers for youth to study in small cubicles on the other side of the store, however, she had loaded up the equipment the day before. She'd put off packing for a week now, still in disbelief of the eviction notice she'd received.

"Brynleigh? Are you still there?"

Brynleigh's heart raced. Smoke wafted through the bi-fold doors.

"I smell smoke. I think the store is on fire. Please. I've got to get out now." She moved closer to the door. The smoke, thicker here, made it difficult to breathe. Long tendrils of red gold hair fell across her eyes, loosened from its clip. Brynleigh pulled the waist of her sweatshirt up to her mouth, her eyes accosted by the acrid smoke.

"Okay, sending Fire now. I think you do need to move. Can you wrap your face up? Touch the door before you open it. Is it hot?"

Her instincts told her to go, despite the fear, and Brynleigh burst through the bi-fold doors into the workroom without obeying the instructions. The outer area filled with smoke, and she could hear the crackling fire in the front room, eating away at her precious books. Brynleigh tripped over the box she'd been packing before the breaking glass and shadowy figure had sent her scurrying to the closet. Falling hard, she smacked her face on a table and crashed to the floor. She whimpered. Would the fire department reach her in time? Coughing hard, Brynleigh pushed up to her knees and put her sleeve over her mouth. That way to the back door, right? The fire, advancing fast, gobbled every paper, book, and combustible item in its way. Brynleigh could feel the heat in the floor as the fire raced to her.

A large, wet nose rammed into her face. What…?

"Grab onto him. He'll guide you out." A male voice cut through the terrifying noise.

A rescue dog with the fire department?

Brynleigh sunk her hands into the shaggy dog's fur and stumbled to the back door.

"That's it. I got you." The man grabbed her and pulled both her and the dog out into the night air.

Tears coursed down her face. Brynleigh looked over her shoulder at her precious bookstore. Crumbling into a heap by the half wall in the alley, Brynleigh saw the red and blue lights of the fire truck and police bouncing off the windows of the other stores. A smattering of water reached her, and she scooted farther into the alley, away from the fire. The big dog, panting, lay down beside her.

She wrapped her arms around her knees and looked up at the man who pulled her out. "Thank you for coming." What a stupid thing to say. Of course, they came. She'd called 911.

"I…uh…" the man stood over her, silhouetted by the flashing lights behind him. She couldn't see his face except for the outline of his ball cap.

"I'm grateful for you rescuing me." She patted the dog. "And you. I didn't know the fire department used dogs now for rescues." The man's wide shoulders were backlit by the fire dancing off the scene behind him.

"Come on, Bandit." The man whistled low. "Time to go."

"Okay, well, thanks." She hugged the dog as he lumbered to a standing position and side-swiped her with his tongue.

Brynleigh watched as the two melted into the night. She turned back to the fire. The gallons of water they were spraying on the store would leave her inventory useless and damaged beyond repair. All of her packing and sorting after the eviction notice, given to all the businesses in the little shopping village outside Dallas, had been for naught. All up in smoke, literally for her.

She turned as a fireman and a police officer, badge swinging outside his Dallas PD vest, approached her. How had she gotten out? A big dog. Did she know the name of the man who had saved her? They'd need his side of the story. No, she didn't. Sorry. She had no idea. He wore a flannel shirt and jeans and had disappeared that way with his dog.

~

Colton Bruens walked back to his truck, a lifted black Dodge, with Bandit by his side. He frowned as he turned the key in the ignition and loud, heavy bass music poured into the cab. He turned down the volume. The normal decibel, which drowned the other things in his head, now felt too loud after the sirens, men shouting, and the roar of the fire. The quiet, not a normal sound he enjoyed, filled the truck and he unclenched his hands from the steering wheel.

"Why do I get involved?"

Bandit's ears perked up.

Colton eyed the can of tobacco on the dash. He really needed to quit. One of the many vices he'd kept after his medical discharge from the Army. Colton grabbed the bottle of pain relievers instead and dropped four into his mouth. Chasing them with the now-warm Monster drink, Colton contemplated his next move. His last shift as night watchman of the shopping village wouldn't be over until 7am.

When the letter came in his meager paycheck envelope, Colton hadn't been surprised the big city of Dallas thought building a hotel in its place was progress. Money hungry developers saw no benefit to community activities, only dollar signs. And to that end, the little shopping area, and his job, came to a close.

Colton drove around the corner and parked along the curb of the cobblestone road. There were still people milling around. The lady he'd sent Bandit in to find stood in the midst of a group of police officers, a heavy blanket thrown across her shoulders. Tall, if not taller, than many of the men, her hair had fallen around her face, curling around her shoulders. Beautiful despite the soot and tracks of mascara from her tears. She must be the owner although he'd never seen her before tonight. So sad, seeing the bookstore go up in flames.

Returning to home base, better known as the tourist tram's housing, Colton settled in for the rest of the night. He'd walk a couple more rounds in an hour and then it would be shift over.

He couldn't wait to wash the smoke off his body and out of his clothes. The worst to wash out, it clung to every inch and squatted there, never intending to leave. Colton took off his hat and ran his fingers through sweaty hair. He'd let it grow long and wild, in defiance of the military's rigid clean-cut policy.

"You stink, too, you know." Colton rubbed Bandit's ears. His fur was matted and gross. Similar to when Bandit tore through bombed villages dragging Colton behind, squeezing around still-smoking wood huts with sparks singeing his coat. Colton's service record had been splattered with moments of heroism and defiance and he'd been constantly at odds with his lieutenant. His saving grace? His lieutenant believed him to be loyal to his squad, treating them better than he did himself, and fearless. More like anger dressed up like fearlessness with no reason to care. What he wore to cover the real issues. As long as the guys he led were safe and completed their mission, he couldn't care less what happened. Until his discharge… along with his dog's. Colton's injury had also been Bandit's injury and they'd both been discharged. Took him completely out of action. And made his life pointless. What good was he stateside? Nope, not going there. Colton eyed the tobacco can again.

The hour drug on to his final walk-through.

"Last pass." Colton told Bandit as he snapped the leash on. Walking slowly around the square for the final time, he noted all of the vacant stores. The courtyard stood empty and dark in the center. Bandit whined when they came close to where the fire had been. Debris layered the ground from the firetrucks and the now burnt store. Bandit continued to whine and ran around to the back, forcing Colton to keep up.

The lady he saved with Bandit's help drug things out the back of the bookstore under the yellow hazard tape. What in the world? She dropped to her knees when she noticed Bandit and hugged him.

"What are you doing?"

The lady swept her long hair over her shoulder. "I had to get some things." She stood, with her fingers still in Bandit's fur.

"Your place just burned down. You can't take things out until the investigator looks it all over."

"Who are you, anyway?"

Colton blew out a breath. They had a saying amongst his buddies, and he'd violated it. Don't feed the animals. Do not engage in conversation. He'd engaged. Pretty alluring, covered in soot and confrontational despite the tear-stained face, she stood with hands on her hips. He hesitated. "I'm the night watchman. Or was."

"You lose your job, too, with the new hotel deal?"

Colton nodded.

"How did you know I was in there?"

"The lights were on when I did my earlier patrol. Figured you were doing some last- minute packing."

"Did you see who broke into my store?"

"What?" Colton frowned. He hadn't noticed

anyone skulking around. "Why would they want to break into your store? You were leaving, right? Not preparing to handcuff yourself to a bookshelf and protest, were you?" Oops. He caught her disgusted look.

"What do you take me for? A protestor? I protested, alright, but it fell on deaf ears."

Colton raised his eyebrows. Feisty…and mad.

"Did. You. See. Who. Broke. Into. My. Store?" She repeated.

"You had a fire. No one broke into your store."

The lady clamped her lips up tight.

"Maybe I'm missing something?"

"Thanks for saving me." She went into the store, dismissing him. He could hear her banging something large through the room.

"Wait. It's really not safe."

"Then help me get this out and I'll be gone."

"Okay, okay." He stepped into the back room and met a very large metal knight. "What the heck?"

"It's a Roman soldier's armor. Now grab the top and back out."

A full-sized set of armor, covered in black soot and still warm to the touch. "Can I ask why this is so important that you'd risk your life, and mine I might add, plus it's probably illegal to remove anything before the investigator comes in?"

"Do you care?"

"Nope, never mind." Colton helped her stand the armor up next to her car. "I don't think that's going to fit."

"It will. Even if I have to cut it in two."

Colton watched as she tried to maneuver the

metal statue into the car. Bandit cocked his head at her efforts.

"Look, it's almost daylight. The inspector will be here later this morning. Can I help?"

"Are you going to cut it in two?" She shot at him.

"No, but I have a truck and I can haul it wherever you need. Within reason." Don't feed the animals. Don't feed the animals. Too late.

Chapter Two

Absurd, allowing this complete stranger to follow her home and learn where she lived. Even though he'd saved her. She could count the number of reasons why she'd agreed on one hand. Good looking man, cool dog. She really wanted that metal soldier and had disregarded the voice in her head suggesting negative consequences.

Pulling down her street, old and quaint, she admired her house as she drove up the tree-lined driveway. Set back from the road, the modest, clean lines of the home stood out amongst the backdrop of trees. The red door and white rocking chairs balanced beautifully with the dark wood of the porch. Her crepe myrtle tree looked stunning this time of year with its large clumps of red flowers.

Brynleigh watched as he turned his truck around in the small circular driveway, backing up to her garage. She stepped out of her car as he opened his truck door.

"Wow. Nice place." He moved around her to see the front.

"Thanks, I like it." Opening the tailgate, she attempted to slide the coat of armor out. "I can take it the rest of the way."

Colton stood with his arms crossed, watching.

"I…um…don't want to scratch your truck."

"It's a work truck and already scratched." Colton pulled the armor-clad statue out of the bed. "Where do you want it?"

"Up on the porch is fine. I'll move it inside later." No way she would let him in her house. Dumb for letting him follow her home, but not stupid enough to invite him in. Especially at eight in the morning. "I don't have much cash on me…" At his puzzled look, which looked just as attractive as his hero look or his baffled one, she pointed to the armor statue. "For gas."

"Lady, I don't want your money. I'm just being nice. You've had quite the last twelve hours."

"Nobody does anything for free. I'll just get my purse. Hang on."

As she reached into her car for her purse, she caught the man starting to pull out of her driveway. He wanted to leave without being paid. Unbelievable.

A delivery truck pulled across her driveway, effectively blocking his escape.

Smugly, she stepped in front of his truck and intercepted the delivery man. He would just have to wait now. Signing for three large, flat boxes, the delivery guy laid them at her feet.

"Do you need help?" The man stepped back out of his truck.

"No, just don't run over them as you race away."

"I wasn't- Never mind." He picked up two of

the boxes and started up the driveway towards the house. "Are you going to pay me?"

Brynleigh spun around, mouth gaping. How rude.

"I was kidding. Look, I'm being helpful. I'm not asking to be paid. I don't even know your name. You know all those signs that say 'be kind'? That's what I'm doing."

"Oh." Maybe not so rude after all. "It's Brynleigh."

"What?"

"My name is Brynleigh."

"Colton." He set the boxes down by the tin man and turned to shake her hand.

"Thank you. You have been very helpful." She shook his hand.

After a long look at her, he nodded and climbed into his truck.

Brynleigh stood on the porch as he drove away. Dragging the coat of armor in the front door and standing it up in the entryway, she thought about the best place to stash it. She would likely scream when she came downstairs in the morning and caught a glance of the tall figure lurking in her home.

Shedding the smelly clothes, Brynleigh jumped in the shower and allowed the perfumed soap and shampoo to wash the smoke stench from her body.

Colton. What a nice name. Manly with wide shoulders, longish hair, hero, kind, to use his words, aggravatingly aloof. She wondered what he'd do now that he wouldn't be the night watchman anymore. Or what she'd do without the bookstore. Owning her own business had been a joy, with the bonus of being involved in the community, a part of something bigger and valuable.

Completely different than how she'd felt working for the family business. She'd gotten the appropriate degrees, interned under the best and brightest in her grandfather's eyes and shadowed her mother often, learning the ropes. Her mother was a force to be reckoned with, just as her grandfather had been, and so on through a long line of family members. They were all power hungry, some would call them cut-throat, but the prestige and bottom dollar led them to early graves. Brynleigh's grandfather had died younger than he should have, but not before handing the reins over to his ambitious daughter. It was not discussed openly, however, Bryleigh's mother expected Brynleigh to do the same. The attitude and antics needed to reach the top of the power grid did not interest Brynleigh in the least. Her mother could have it all. She had disappointed her mother when Brynleigh broke free of the corporate world and started out on her own to find purpose and direction for her life. The bookstore had been just the ticket. She could use her business sense to make the bookstore successful and provide a place for community activities. Win-win situation.

Thinking of her mother reminded Brynleigh the boxes delivered had been from her. Brynleigh pulled the bow off the top one and slid a shocking blue dress out of the box. Floor length and stunning. The second box held a pale pink chiffon number with a plunging neckline. What in the world was her mother up to? The final one had an off-the-shoulder maxi length black dress with exquisite beadwork sewn into the bodice. Elegant and beautiful.

Brynleigh dialed her mother's phone and set the boxes off to the side. "Mother." She could picture her mother in a white leather chair in her castle, drinking white wine and thinking up ways to stay the most powerful woman in Dallas.

"Oh, Brynleigh, you probably received the dresses. Aren't they divine?"

"Mother, you know I did. I had to sign for them. What are they for?"

"Why, the gala, of course. You pick which one you like and simply send the rest back. I'll send a car for you Saturday night around 6pm."

"I'm not going to any gala. You know I hate that stuff. Mother, my bookstore-" Brynleigh started, but like every other time she tried to tell her mother something important, she talked over her like she hadn't spoken a word.

"I will not take no for an answer. You will put one of those dresses on, the pink one will match my dress perfectly, and be ready on time."

Definitely not the pink one. "Martha," that should get her attention.

"Do not call me Martha. You may call me Celeste, or Mother, if you are feeling kind, but never, ever call me that."

"Then listen to me, Celeste. Mother. My store-" Her mother had once again hung up on her.

~

Colton pulled through the cattle gate and parked next to the two story, old farmhouse. A newer house sat farther back, surrounded by out buildings. Although his aunt and brother had remodeled the newer house's living quarters and moved in, he could still feed the ghosts and skeletons scratching on the closet doors, reminding him of his terrible childhood. He normally joined the family for breakfast in the newly expanded kitchen after his night shifts, however, Colton didn't think his aunt would allow him in the door smelling like he did.

"You'll have to wait for a bath." Colton fed Bandit in the farmhouse's kitchen and then moved up the creaky stairs to his modest bedroom with adjoining bathroom. He'd taken over the old farmhouse after his discharge, refusing to sleep under the same roof that he had grown up in. His aunt and brother could have the newer house. He peeled off his shirt and tossed his remaining clothes in the corner. His pants and shirt were covered in soot from the tin man statue.

Brynleigh.

Pretty lady.

He smiled, thinking about her attempts to load the armor guy into her car. Determined, he'd give her that. And a little stubborn. Her green eyes were red from the smoke and her cheeks were shadowed by her tears.

When he'd grabbed her and pulled them both out through the door, he'd expected a slight frame, but he'd been mistaken. Solid and athletic, he noticed as her long hair wound itself over his shoulder.

Colton shook his hair, sending droplets of water across the bathroom. She was pretty to look at but he had no room in his life for females. Putting on a different flannel shirt, Colton got in his truck and headed to the main house. He stopped in the gravel outside the ranch-style home, popped a couple more pain killers in his mouth and swallowed without water.

"Those are going to kill you someday." Mark, Colton's younger brother greeted him on the porch.

"Ibuprofen? Better than the alternative. Could be meth or marijuana or the granddaddy of them all, fentanyl." Colton couldn't resist taunting him. "It's like a pre-breakfast snack. Besides, if Pop couldn't kill me and the Afghans couldn't, you think Ibuprofen will?"

Mark followed him into the house. Knocking a sofa leg with his knee, Colton clamped his lips down on a curse. He straightened, gritted his teeth, and moved toward the smell of bacon.

"Aunt Eunice moved the furniture around again," Mark commented behind him.

The pain shooting up his leg to his thigh told him that news.

"Good morning." Colton greeted his aunt. "Sorry I'm later than normal."

"Ah, there's plenty. The boys haven't eaten yet either. Mark, you can call them now."

Colton grabbed a plate and loaded up with pancakes and bacon. Mark whistled out the back door.

"Eggs, Colton. You need the protein. You are too skinny." Aunt Eunice pushed spoonfuls of scrambled eggs onto his plate.

Colton looked down at his waist. Not skinny by any stretch of imagination. Well, maybe his aunt's. Being discharged from the Army with an injury may have whittled down his figure a little, but he was not skinny. Colton balanced the mug of coffee on his plate and hesitated as Mark prayed over the food.

Taking a spot on the wrought iron picnic bench out back where he could see in all directions, Colton watched as the boys, ranging in height and age, came out of the various outbuildings. Mark had opened the ranch to troubled youth ten years ago after their father went to prison for laying his hands on their mother too many times. Colton crossed himself. He never went into parts of the main house where memories of his father assaulting his mother with his fists would crash in his head. Aunt Eunice had come when their mother had died of breast cancer. Anger and hate colored most corners of the house for Colton. However, Aunt Eunice and Mark threw up brightly painted pictures, flowers, and live plants to change the landscape from a dark environment to a peaceful one. All of the emotions he felt growing up in the house settled over their attempts like a gravesite with bones below and decorated floral arrangements above. Colton could even now feel his gut turn and the anger start to burn. He started to pull out more Ibuprofen, when he heard Bandit give a low growl.

"I do not like your dog." The teenage boy, dressed all in black with black fingernail polish, stood looking at him with a steaming plate of breakfast.

"Clearly, the feeling's mutual." Colton put a hand on Bandit.

"Colton, this is Billy, our newest resident. Billy, Colton, my brother. Have a seat." Mark went around Billy and sat across from Colton.

"No." Billy took his food and went under a shade tree to eat.

Colton raised eyebrows at Mark who shrugged his shoulders and forked in a big bite of pancakes. The boys were court-ordered to be at the ranch, with the alternative of going straight to juvenile detention. They were all here for different reasons, some because of their parents' decisions, all because they were steps from entering the justice system. Mark had a big heart for them all, but Colton, well, he lived by the 'you get what you give' rule. There hadn't been anyone around or interested when their father beat up their mother. It was up to the brothers to make the most of their life, for what it was worth. His brother received a generous nature, patience, and compassion from their mother. Colton got his father's anger.

"Listen, I have some things I'm hoping you could help with." Mark started, after a brief moment of silence.

"Well, seeing that I don't have a job anymore…" Colton trailed off. "Sorry. My knee is killing me, I lost a job, it's just not been easy. Sorry."

"I know. I really believe it will get better. Somehow."

"Maybe." Colton knew his brother was trying. Just so much water under the bridge. "What do you need help with?"

"Tagging the livestock. The boys will help."

"Him, too?" Colton glanced over at Billy.

"Yep, everyone has a part."

"Think he can handle the cattle? He's tall, but scrawny."

"It's goats. And calves, but mostly goats."

Colton pushed back from the table. "Oh, nuh, uh. I'm not doing anything with goats. Nasty, vile creatures."

"What?"

"Look, this is what we did to goats." Colton pulled his phone out, swiped through some pictures and showed the screen to Mark.

"You're feeding the goat? Or horse? Or what is that thing? It's huge."

"It's a goat. And yes, we're feeding it. Poisoned bread. I know, I know, you probably think that's horrible." Colton swiped a hand across his brow and closed the phone. "You wouldn't understand. Goats in Afghanistan, and many middle eastern cultures, are considered tokens of greatness and excellence. This one Afghanistan guy loved his goat as much as he hated us Americans. He'd take his goat out for a stroll and start firing on us, using the goat as a shield. So, we killed his goat."

"A revenge thing." Mark rocked back on the picnic bench. "But all goats?"

"I'm not proud of it. Nor can I explain it. I just hate goats now. Trust me, I will not work with goats. I'll do the calves, but never the goats."

"Have you seen the goats? They're fainting goats. They'd fall over in fright if you…" Mark's sentence drifted off. "Okay, you do the calves. But you get Billy, too."

"Great. One exchange for another."

"It'll be fun." Mark and Colton picked up their plates and returned them to the kitchen.

"It'll be fun, he says," Colton mimicked over

his shoulder. "Come on, Billy, and you and you." Colton pointed out a couple of other boys and walked to the cow shed.

Colton showed them how to load the calves, bawling for their mothers, into the chutes, load the tag gun, and puncture the ear. A simple effective way to identify the cattle and who they belonged to. Colton knew his brother was teaching Bible lessons to the others who were tagging the goats. His objective? Do the job effectively and efficiently, help his brother, and then sleep the rest of the day. No time for cute Bible lessons.

"Doesn't that hurt their ears?" one of the younger teenagers asked.

Billy snorted. "Did it hurt yours?"

Colton looked up at his tone and back at the boy who had spoken. Sure enough, the boy had wide holes in both ears held open by what looked like rubber circles. Kid had a point.

"Shut up, Billy."

"Sure thing, boy with a girl's name." Billy taunted.

"Look who's talking, boy with the nail polish."

"Okay, stop. Let's just get this done." Colton looked over the top of the chute and caught Billy's dead-pan gaze. Just a well of anger stacking up. He knew that feeling. Also knew, at some point, the well would implode.

After an hour of silent work, they were done, and Billy and Colton were the only ones left in the barn.

A large hawk swooped low from the rafters searching for an opening, clearly disturbed by the activity in the pens. Colton felt the rush of air and dropped to the ground, face first on the dirt floor. Billy dropped, too, just to his right. Colton's heart sped up like a locomotive and he put his hands behind his neck, covering his head. Every inch of his body quaked. Sweat dropped into the dirt.

"What is happening?" Billy's head on his arms muffled his voice.

No response. Colton tried to form words, but they stuck in his head, unable to move from his brain to his lips. Silently, he counted 1, 2, 3, 4…1, 2, 3, 4.

The two of them laid on the floor for another couple of minutes until Billy rose, shaking the dirt off his jeans.

Echoes of another time faded at the sound of the kid moving beside him. Realizing he was still in his brother's cow barn and not in a war-torn village, he muttered, "I'm okay. I'm okay. I'm okay." Scrambling up, neither spoke as they made their way back to the house.

Chapter Three

Brynleigh pushed the doorbell at the side of the tall, wooden doors. She could hear the chimes echo through the mansion. She termed it the castle, with its wide turrets and expansive lawn. Other people called it the 'house on the hill' as it overlooked the majority of the Dallas area.

"Good morning, Brynleigh. I wasn't expecting you to drop by. Did you choose a dress?" Celeste led her into the 'white room'. This is where she imagined her mother most of the time, propped up against white pillows on the white couch with her designer clothes, surveying her kingdom every morning. Ostentatious with a variety of textures, feathers, and cold tile, the entertaining room held the most stunning view of the city. Brynleigh never grew up in this house, she had her own home when she was twenty and as far removed from her mother's monstrosity as possible.

"No. I'm not going. The dresses are lovely, but I won't be wearing them. They're out in the car."

"Of course, you're going. Don't be silly. This is part of me being your mother. You attend the events I tell you to. I haven't asked much of you since you left the company, but you do owe me for all my time and energy."

"I'm sorry, owe you for what?" Brynleigh tried to lower her voice.

"Dear, I spent a lot of money making sure you were comfortable in your job at the company and then a lot of energy staying out of your way when you wanted to own your own business and started that musty little bookstore. You could have had so much." Celeste waved her perfectly manicured hand at the things in the room.

Brynleigh blinked. She should not have come. She was no match for her mother and what she wanted, she got. Regardless of how. Persuasive, intimidating, conniving... Brynleigh's brain spun with all of the adjectives.

Holding up her own non-manicured hand, Brynleigh stopped her mother. "Why is it so important I attend this gala? You haven't forced me to go to any others. Not since I worked for you at least."

"Because I'm ill."

"Ill as in mad at me? Or ill as in sick?"

"As in sick. I may be dying."

Brynleigh rolled her eyes. Of all the stunts to pull...

"You may not believe me, but I am. You have all the skills needed to run the company in my absence. I trained you, gave you all the tools you will need."

"What? What are you talking about? Your absence?" Brynleigh's voice raised two octaves. "And prove it. Why are you dying exactly?"

"Lower your voice. You do not need to shout

at me. You are such an obstinate child. I went to my normal annual exam, and the doctor said she found something."

"Who's the doctor? That's it? She found something? What does that even mean?"

Brynleigh followed her mother into the kitchen.

Celeste reached up into a high cabinet and pulled down a basket of medication. Taking one bottle out, she read the prescription "Dr. A. H. Beck".

It looked legit, but her mother was a smart cookie and oh, so conniving. Opening her phone, she looked up Dr. A. H. Beck. An oncologist specializing in breast cancer.

"Now do you believe me?"

Celeste did look paler than usual. Brynleigh backed up a step. Vulnerable was not a descriptor for her mother and yet, there very well could be something wrong with her. Brynleigh frowned. "No. I don't. I'll be talking with this Dr. Beck. Go back to the leave of absence part."

"I'm taking time off from the corporation, and you will be sitting temporarily in my place."

"Oh no I won't. That is not happening. I left for a good reason."

"Brynleigh, while I appreciate your need to run your own business," her mother's voice dripped sweet like hot honey, the bite about to surface, "it's time for you to come back to your senses and run the family business for a time. You are needed, and it's what your grandfather would have wanted."

"I'm not. There's nothing you can say that will make me go back to the corporation, or run it in your absence."

"Remind me…what were you saying about your little bookstore? It burned down, did it not?" Ah, the predicted bite.

"After I got evicted. So someone, like this corporation, could build a hotel. Crazy coincidences, aren't they?"

"I don't know what you are insinuating. If you do this for me, I will buy you another bookstore."

"Right. Why me? Why not one of your devoted vice presidents?"

"Because you are family, and this is family run. Has been for decades. Now, go pick a dress and be ready for my car to pick you up." Celeste gestured with her diamond-studded hand. Time for Brynleigh to go.

"This conversation isn't over by a long shot." Brynleigh didn't miss the smirk on her mother's face. She needed to think, somewhere outside of Celeste's realm of power, about everything that had been said. Going to the gala wouldn't change anything. Her mother being ill wouldn't be a factor. The promise of a bookstore at her mother's expense might be. Worth time in painful subservience to the corporation, though? She understood the reason her mother wanted Brynleigh in the president's seat, not the stated one of the corporation being a family-run business, but the unstated one- her mother believed she could control Brynleigh. Maybe she could, at least until the new bookstore was purchased.

~

Colton pulled the shades down farther to block the sunlight pouring in around the old windows.

After a night shift, he'd usually been asleep for a couple of hours by now. Tossing and turning in the old metal bed someone had found in the attic, Colton groaned and took more Ibuprofen. His leg burned all the way from his ankle to his thigh and if this pain killer didn't kick in, he'd take a different one. No reason to lay in bed, writhing in pain, when the stronger meds were in the drawer across the room. They were too potent to leave on his nightstand and accidentally eat a handful.

Bandit snored on his side of the bed. His long torso stretched to full length, his paws quivering as he chased rabbits, he was like having another body in the bed.

Colton wished he could doze off that quick, however, images of a tall red head trying to push a six-foot-tall tin man into her car worked their way through his consciousness.

Brynleigh.

Grimacing, Colton rolled over. He'd never been good with women, always comparing them to his mother. He knew his mom took blows from his father so he wouldn't turn on him and his brother, but he never understood why she didn't snatch the boys up and run. And he prayed fervently he would never, ever, be like his father. His anger welled up inside often enough. Never, ever would he lay a finger on any woman despite how she may infuriate him. He would never be that kind of monster.

His thoughts swung back to Brynleigh.

Maybe she set the fire for the insurance money. Colton sat up in bed. There's a thought. What had she said about someone breaking in before the fire started? Just out of curiosity, he might have to swing back by the village and the now-burnt bookstore.

Hearing crashing sounds outside his window, Colton shrugged off any more attempts to sleep and went downstairs to his kitchen. A strong cup of coffee, or several, were what he needed now.

He put the black coffee into a mug and stepped outside to see what had caused the racket. At the back of the barn, he found the source as a flying baseball narrowly missed him. Another crash drew his eyes to the bottles lined up against a low running wall. Sunlight glinted off shards of broken glass.

Billy, the black clad teenager who had helped with the calves, stood poised with baseball in hand, more ammunition at his feet.

"What?" Billy gritted through his teeth, a sheen of tears in his eyes.

"Didn't know what the commotion was." Colton leaned back against the barn wall. "You know what the problem is?"

"Don't care."

Colton knew that feeling.

"I'll clean it up."

Colton hesitated, not sure if the kid would take the chance to bean him or not and walked over to the line of bottles. Billy tossed the baseball back and forth from hand to hand. Moving two of the bottles from the base of the brick wall up to the top of the wall, Colton gingerly made his way through the broken glass. "Where'd you get all these bottles?"

Silence.

Colton stepped back to the barn, slightly behind Billy.

Billy nodded at the rearranged bottles. "What's your point?"

"No point. Just thought you should set them at the strike zone."

Billy let another fly, connecting to a bottle in a dead aim and dropping it to the pile below with a sufficient crash. He sent the second loose with the same result.

"Wow, that's a really good shot."

"So?"

"Have you ever played ball before?"

"No."

"Ever been coached?"

"No." Billy slanted his eyes at Colton. "What's with all the questions?"

"What's your name again, kid?"

"Why?"

"Just asking."

"Billy."

"Like 'Billy, the…'?" Colton stopped when the kid turned and raised his arm as if to launch the ball at Colton's head. "Whoa, dude."

Billy glared at him for a moment and then set up more bottles on the top of the wall like Colton had. Walking back to the barn, the kid wouldn't meet his eyes.

Colton picked up a ball and winged it at one of the bottles, dropping it just as neatly as Billy had.

"Dude, you almost hit me." Billy ducked.

"I did not. Get out of the way." Colton threw another ball at the bottles, just missing them. The ball ricocheted off the wall and bounced back to them. Billy grabbed it with his bare hands. "You don't have a glove?"

Billy cursed, using God's name in vain.

"Hey, don't do that."

"What, say…" Billy said it again.

"Look, it's just not right."

"So, you'd rather I say…" Billy used a string of four-letter words that would have made anybody but Colton blush.

Colton laughed out loud, startling the kid. "Yes, use those words if you must, but keep God's name out of your mouth."

"Why? He hates me. Why do I care?" Billy spit on the ground.

"I'm pretty sure that's not true, but why do you think that?" Colton licked his lips. He was talking religion with this kid?

"What's the glove got to do with anything?"

"This." Colton lobbed the ball at Billy who caught it and lightning fast, turned and busted another bottle. Colton whistled his appreciation. "Why do you hate God?"

Billy spread his arms wide indicating everything around him. "This is jail, homie."

"Oh, I get it. You think God hates you which is why you're living in the country with fresh air, three square meals, wide open spaces. Yeah, that's rough, homie."

"Shut up, dude. You don't know anything about me."

True. And this kid didn't know anything about Colton either.

"It's like you've got it pretty good here. My brother takes care of everyone well."

"Your brother, the jailor?"

"That's not very fair."

"Life's not fair. Didn't they teach you that in your rich boy classes?" Billy dropped the ball in his hand and walked away.

He thought Colton was rich? Maybe from the boy's perspective. Wouldn't have been the first time his brother had mentioned the horrible living conditions some of the boys had grown up in.

Colton tried to shake the conversation with Billy, but it sounded ungrateful even in his head. He did have it pretty good, considering. The God talk bothered him more. He didn't believe God hated him. Didn't know he existed or indifferent to the choices Colton made was more like it. If he stayed out of God's way, then God could stay out of his way, too. His brother would have introduced a Bible story or taught a great lesson on how good God was. His brother could believe that, but Colton had seen too much and done too much to believe God was good.

Colton drifted off in a fitful sleep in his hand-me-down recliner, with the TV on a dopey house building show. Hours later, he struggled to his feet, took another shower and fixed a meager meal of leftovers.

Colton, deep in thought, rubbed Bandit's ears. At some point, he wanted to go back to the shopping center and check out the burnt bookstore again. He doubted there'd be anything more for him to see than when he'd left her last, dragging out the armor, but he had the time. It had been, after all, his job to watch over the stores in the area at night and if what she said was true, someone had snuck in under his radar.

Chapter Four

Brynleigh hated riding in her mother's company car. Luxurious black leather seats cradled her in just the right spots and a small cooler sat between the seats which she knew held a variety of drinks, from alcoholic to diet. The driver, polite and formal, had helped her sweep the chosen black dress into the back seat. It wasn't the car that bothered Brynleigh, it was the over-the-top, this-money-could-be-used-so-very-differently luxury. Brynleigh's store had been vastly different from this showcase of wealth.

She looked down at her hands. Gloves were all the glam nowadays, however, she'd left hers in the box, opting for silver bangles and a stacked layer of diamonds. More diamonds glittered her ears and fingers. Some real, some not- Brynleigh didn't care as long as they matched the simplistic elegance of the gown.

She took a deep breath. Why did she give in to her mother and agree to attend the gala? Again. She gave in again. Celeste got her way and did it with as much pomp and circumstance as possible. Was she really sick? Who knew? The meds seemed legit, and the doctor was definitely a real doctor. Brynleigh didn't trust Celeste one ounce, because Celeste didn't do anything without a motive. The unknown reason behind the urgency for Brynleigh to attend tonight and despite the hated, but expected, manipulation, she'd resigned herself to take her mother's offer and attend. A new bookstore would be worth it, she hoped.

Leaving the warmth of the car, Brynleigh admired all the twinkling lights outside the mansion-turned-event space. An enchanted evening theme wound its way into the large foyer complete with a waterfall and enormous floral arrangements. The ballroom completed the concept with a sea of snowy white tablecloths, black accents and gold silverware.

"Sweetheart, we're up here." Celeste greeted her in a tight turquoise number with feathers around the collar and guided her to a table up front. Of course. Center of attention. Brynleigh fully expected a throne to be sitting up on the low stage.

Sweetheart? Ugh.

"Introduce yourselves. I'll be back in a moment."

Seated in between two of the other company members, Brynleigh took a sip of water.

"Good evening. I'm Lucas Woodspin, Vice President of Texas Acquisitions and Development Corporation." The man took her hand in his.

A good firm handshake and a handsome face, this seat may not be so bad. "Brynleigh Tavish."

"I figured you must be the daughter if Celeste seated you with us."

Brynleigh looked at her plate for a second

before raising her eyes to his. "I am." Let's establish that fact right up front. Normally, she wouldn't connect herself to Celeste Tavish, but here they were and by Lucas' tone, he might need reminding.

Her dinner companion on the other side snorted quietly. Brynleigh turned to her and offered her hand. "And you are?"

"Juliette, ma'am."

"Please don't call me that. So formal." Brynleigh waved her hands around. "This isn't the place to be formal now, is it?"

Juliette coughed into her napkin, her gray eyes twinkling.

"Brynleigh. And what do you do at Texas A&D?" Brynleigh smiled at her.

"I'm a Vice President, too."

"Ah, two vice presidents and I'm privileged enough to sit in between both."

Brynleigh smelled a rat.

Juliette put her hand on Brynleigh's arm. "That dress looks magical on you."

"So does yours." Brynleigh sized up her new acquaintance. Voluptuous and beautiful, she made Brynleigh's athletic frame feel not-so-curvy. Juliette's genuine personality seemed at odds with all of the fakeness around them, endearing her to Brynleigh quickly.

Lucas, on the other hand, tapped his fingers on the table incessantly, and she wondered if she would be able to stand listening to it all night without slapping his knuckles.

With the meal served, he quieted his drumming. Plates of thick bread and chilled butter were passed around as were the salad dressings. Servers in starched uniforms laid plates of chicken and garlic potatoes, asparagus and fancy vegetables at each setting. Her mother's plate stayed clean as if the staff knew she would not be eating the meal with them. *Wonder where she's at. Probably schmoozing with other VP's across the room.*

"Lucas, how long have you been with Texas A&D?"

Lucas livened up a little and engaged Brynleigh with stories of early years with her mother.

"You've been with the corporation awhile now, it sounds like."

"Your mother took me in and taught me all the ropes."

She bet. With Lucas' good looks, she suspected many women had difficulty not attaching themselves to him, including her mother. However, she also knew Celeste to be shrewd and not keep someone around simply because of their looks. They must be an asset in other ways.

"And what about you, Juliette?" Catching a smirk on Juliette's face at Lucas' last comment, Brynleigh held her gaze.

"Several years. I was an attorney on one of your mother's lawsuits and she thought I'd be a good fit for Texas A&D, so she brought me on. I have both a law degree and an MBA."

"Wow, that's amazing. I guess she knows a good thing when she sees it." Brynleigh licked her lips. Her own attendance at the gala, fraught with strings and dangling carrots, would be a good thing in her mother's eyes. The pressure mounted around her, almost stifling. The climax of the evening, her mother's address to the stakeholders, could not come fast enough. Would she share she was ill? Or keep the information to herself? Would that show her as being weak or smart, pulling on emotions?

They had not discussed anything past Celeste's leave of absence and the new bookstore carrot. Brynleigh planned to give her mother an answer next week after the gala.

"Good evening, ladies and gentlemen. I trust you enjoyed your meal." Celeste took center stage. The feathers around the neckline of her dress danced with her every movement.

Okay, here goes.

"Just a little business before we get into the fun things."

Blah, blah, blah. Brynleigh picked at her nails. Okay, yes, you made lots of money. Yes, thank all of the little people and the big ones seated here after serving a $500 plate. Yes, you, of course, have multiple projects in the works. Wait. Winslot project? B's Books was located in the Winslot Shopping Village. Before the fire. The screen behind her mother moved on to other land acquisitions and building projects. Could her mother's company be behind the leveling of the village? Brynleigh tried to remember what the eviction notice had said. It had burned up in the fire so no way she could confirm. Brynleigh's hair on her arms began to quiver. Definitely something to talk to her mother about in the near future. So help her if she was behind crashing Brynleigh's dreams.

"And now to the most important news. Vice

President Mr. Lucas Woodspin and Vice President Miss Juliette Romano, will you please stand?"

Brynleigh stiffened as the two vice presidents stood to her left and right.

"In the last couple of months, these two have been by my side while I encountered health issues and I want to formally thank you for your hard work." Light applause filtered through the ballroom. "You may sit now."

"Brynleigh, will you please stand?"

No, no, no. Whatever her mother had in mind, it was a hard pass. Brynleigh sideswiped a look at Juliette. No eye contact. Brynleigh found herself obeying and pushed away from the table, all eyes on her.

"This is my one and only daughter, Brynleigh Tavish." More applause. "She has worked at Texas Acquisitions and Development Corporation before and learned the business from me directly. She has her grandfather's sense of management and the family's best interest at heart." Celeste paused.

Brynleigh remained standing, rock still, concentrating on her jaw not falling open in shock. No, no, no…please don't do this…she never agreed. To anything. She stared at her mother, willing her to stop talking.

"I will be taking a leave of absence for a brief time while I complete the rest of my medical treatment."

"Oh mys" rang out across the room.

"Brynleigh is entirely capable of running the corporation in my absence along with my two best vice presidents at her side."

Brynleigh's knees buckled. No way. Not a chance. She steadied herself with fingers on the table, a small smile for each of the vice presidents sitting on either side. Juliette looked at her with compassion, Lucas would barely meet her eyes. Brynleigh took a deep breath and turned back to her mother. Of all the manipulative, heartless things her mother had done in the past, this one, this one was aimed directly at Brynleigh. Not only did her mother play the family card, but she also set Brynleigh up to look bad if she refused to take her mother's place while she completed treatment. If she said no, everyone would think Brynleigh was unsympathetic and selfish.

"I will, of course, be available and watchful, expecting this great corporation will continue to grow and prosper." Celeste lifted her arms as if she'd pulled off the best show in town.

And she had.

"Now onto the dessert and entertainment." Servers scurried around, emptying tables of dirty dishes and replacing them with decadent multi-layer cake slices, while a jazz band, the entertainment, played fast ragtime tunes interchanged with slower blues music.

Brynleigh slid back into her seat. Everything looked tarnished, even the table servings and the rich desserts. How could she? Virtually no discussion, no formal acceptance, no consideration, only a blindside. Why was she surprised her mother took the decision out of her hands and made it for her? So she could get what she wanted?

Lucas threw down his napkin and pushed away from the table. He strode away, leaving Brynleigh gaping at his back. Juliette put a hand on her arm, pulling her attention back to the table.

"Not expecting that?" Juliette frowned.

"Uh, no." Brynleigh dabbed her lips with the napkin, certain all of her lipstick had disappeared, like her future. She never wanted to go back into the corporate world. Ever. The purpose of the bookstore, to use her expertise and education to better the community, not build high rises and glitzy casinos, or whatever power move her mother had her hands into, fell apart in the space of an hour.

"Listen, I know you don't know me yet, but I'm on your side. I have more bad news, you're expected to come in on Monday. Your mother set up a meeting first thing. I'm supposed to let you know so we can start the paperwork on the transfer of authority to you."

"Are you kidding me? This is Saturday night. And I'm supposed to take over on Monday?" Nope, this was not happening. Any minute she'd wake from this nightmare.

"Just to get the paperwork started. I'll walk you through most of it and Lucas will do some of it. Your mother will be there for a little bit."

"Oh yeah, I'll have some choice words for her then. I have NONE now." Brynleigh stood. Juliette stood as well.

"I know this is overwhelming. Celeste can be overwhelming. I know. But I don't think she's going to change her mind. Let's go day by day and see where this leads. God may have opened a door for you."

Whew, if this was God, He had a cruel sense of

humor.

"Tell my mother I will see her on Monday. Just maybe not the way she hopes."

Brynleigh scooped up her dress and left the stifling ballroom, praying that she could leave without running into her mother. Ordering her car be brought around, she stood in the night air, allowing the fresh breeze to blow over her. This was a disaster.

~

Colton arrived at the tram station, his former headquarters, and walked back to the burned bookstore, retracing his steps from his last night on the job. The notion that someone had gone under his security radar and set a fire, or possibly broken into Brynleigh's store, had nagged at him all week. He watched from the stoop of the bookstore as a sleek, black car parked on the curb. Interesting. The driver came around to the side, opened the door, and offered his hand to the occupant. A black shiny dress followed the glittery shoes out of the car. The owner of the bookstore emerged, looking like a princess. His sweeping gaze took in the beautiful hair curled precisely at her neck, her curves in all the right places, and the grace with which she exited the vehicle. He paused and tried to catch his breath as her green eyes turned to him. Exquisite. Colton's face heated up and he wiped clammy hands on his pants.

"Hi." Colton took her out-stretched hand and helped her across the sidewalk still littered with debris.

"Hi, back. I didn't expect to see you here." Brynleigh dropped the gown hem.

"I don't know much about these things, but it's

really dirty and your dress is dragging through it all."

Colton eyed her dress. Flattering, stylish. It was some dress. He struggled to not openly ogle her. What the heck was he supposed to be doing?

"After my evening, I couldn't care less what happens to this dress."

"It's very pretty." Pretty? More than pretty, but he couldn't think of any different words. No words. Nothing he forced out of his mouth would make him look any smarter.

"It is, I agree." Brynleigh cocked her head. "You didn't say why you are here."

Colton stared at her, caught in his head.

"Earth to Colton. That is your name, right?"

"Oh, sorry. You look stunning, Miss-"

"Good grief. It's Brynleigh. Not 'Miss'." A smile flitted across her face, lighting up her eyes.

Colton chewed the inside of his lip. Awkward. "Brynleigh." Get ahold of yourself. She was female. All dressed up and smelling very pretty. That's all. "Brynleigh. Yes, of course. Sorry. Something you said made me think about the fire here, so I came to poke around. And then, honestly, you arrived, and I forgot why I was here." Liar. You forgot everything, including your words and your manners.

A full-on smile from Brynleigh. "What did I say?"

"About the fire? Some details about that night that bothered me. You said you had a bad evening tonight. Are you better now?" Colton noticed the napkin wrapped around her finger. Lifting her hand so he could see it better, he gently pulled the paper cloth away from her skin. Little droplets of blood were scattered across the napkin.

"It's nothing. I shred my cuticles when I'm angry."

"Oh. Blood and anger do make for a bad evening," Colton joked and wound the napkin back into her hand.

"Ha, ha. I don't want to talk about what made me angry. What made you think of the fire?"

"You said someone broke into your store before the fire. Why do you think that?"

"I didn't just think it. I called 911 because it happened."

"Is that why you called 911? You were in the store?"

"I started packing when I heard the front door glass break. At first, I wasn't sure about the sound, and then I saw someone move across the front of the store."

Colton held up the Do Not Enter tape left by the police so Brynleigh could stoop under it and enter the shell of the bookstore.

"Do you see where the glass is broken out right here?" Brynleigh faced the door.

Colton turned the flashlight on his phone and grimaced. The whole pane was shattered. "It looks like where the firemen came in through. Both sides are broken."

"That's what everyone else will see, too." She touched the napkin still wound around her finger.

"Do you know why they broke in? Can you tell if anything is missing? Is that why you're here?" Colton watched Brynleigh look around at the sodden bookstore as the light from his phone bounced off sooty walls and burned items. Shelves were sagging in areas where the water had dripped. Books with spines broken and desks overturned were evidence of the full blast of water.

Colton offered his arm to her. Nothing looked stable there, including the warped floorboards. She hooked her hand in his elbow and moved farther into the store. Her touch increased his awareness of their closeness and the heat from her hand on his arm sped up his heart rate. Glass and scorched paper crunched under their feet.

"I don't know why I'm here. Maybe just a reminder of what happened and what next steps I'm considering. I have no idea if anything was taken." She piled several books together and put them neatly on a shelf, leaving a trace of gray, powdery soot on the front of her dress. Tears ran down her beautiful face. Ruined, the whole place.

"Hey." Colton took her hand, his pulse picking up speed again. "Let's go back outside. The air is cool, and I think you need a break from all of this."

"What do you know about me?"

She could have stomped her foot like a three-year-old and he wouldn't have been more surprised. Raising his eyebrows, he continued to hold her hand with his. "Well, for one thing…" He badly wanted to wipe away the tears still coursing down her cheeks, but he didn't know how she would respond. He pulled a Kleenex out of his pocket and handed it to her.

"It's clean," he offered.

She patted her face dry and wiped her nose. Squaring her shoulders, she tried to hand the Kleenex back to him.

Colton laughed. "You can keep it."

What he really wanted to do was shield her from the nightmarish sight of her beloved bookstore up in smoke. What he really, really wanted to do was… Was he kidding? He'd known her all of a couple of hours within the week.

"Come on." Colton pulled her out of the store. "Would you be okay sitting in the courtyard for a bit? I don't think your driver will mind waiting."

"Sure." Brynleigh spoke to the driver and then followed him across the cobblestone street.

Colton intentionally chose a bench facing away from the damaged bookstore. A slight breeze teased the tendrils of hair around her face.

"Let's start over. You heard someone breaking into your store, and you got scared and called 911."

"Wouldn't you? They were in my store."

Colton thought about all of the times he and his squad slid into dark homes or came in loud like banshees. A little different, dude.

He skirted the question. "Why do you think they broke in? Do you think they knew you were there?"

Brynleigh turned to look at him.

"If they knew I was in there, then they purposefully started the fire to hurt me."

Colton watched as she started to shake.

"There's nothing of value in the store for anyone but me."

Colton took her hand, noting her cold fingertips. "Look, the police and fire department were here earlier, and they will both have investigations to complete. Let's not jump to conclusions. Maybe one of the neighborhood kids wanted a book to read." His attempt to alleviate the seriousness of her statement fell flat. "Let the authorities handle this."

"But am I safe?" Brynleigh looked around the dark courtyard. By day, it was usually filled with families strolling through. By night, the streetlamps bounced yellow hazy light on the stores on the other side.

"Yes, you are. Especially with me." Colton released her hand and put his arm around the back of the bench. "Tell me what brought you back to the store tonight. In this finery." Never had he ever been comfortable with a woman or small talk. Foreign land, buddy, foreign land.

"Just something I was coerced into attending. I *really* don't want to talk about that. Let's talk about you."

He *really* didn't want to talk about *that*. What did normal people talk about in a dark lot with a stranger? Chit chat was not his style. Or talking in general. To a female. Colton inwardly groaned. He was so bad at this and yet, he really didn't want the night to end.

"What are you going to do now that the shopping village is closing?" Safe topic.

"Part of this evening, I guess, was about that. I was blindsided, should have seen it coming, but I put too much hope in people. What about you?"

A whole lot of vague. "I've got a few leads out." He could be vague, too.

"A friend and I play this little game when we

go out to dinner. We pick out individuals around us and try to decide what they do for a living. If you saw me out at dinner, what would you think my career was?"

Colton looked at her beautiful face, the diamonds on her ears, her hair simply knotted in back. Brynleigh turned pink under his gaze as she arched one eyebrow.

"You're taking too long."

Colton debated about what was running through his mind. Model. Princess. His. What? "A piano teacher with a secret love for dandelions."

Brynleigh laughed. He hadn't heard a more wonderful sound in so long.

"Yeah, right." She continued to laugh, her shoulders shaking until she was almost crying. "You're next. Hmmm…" Brynleigh stood and pulled him up beside her. She walked a 360 around him.

Colton could feel her dress hem brush over his boots. He stood at parade rest, hands clasped behind his back. He pressed his lips together. This was not good. She was tormenting him, a good torment, but still…

"Okay, easy soldier, I know what you do. Or did."

Colton held his breath. He rarely talked about anything he did during his service in the military.

"I think you're going to be surprised how accurate I'm about to be."

Colton sat when she did, sweat rolling down his back.

"I think you were a boxer who traveled around

on a ship, making gourmet meals for sailors."

He laughed so hard he nearly fell off the bench. He hadn't laughed like that in forever.

"I was in the Army, not Navy, and I did box. I can't cook gourmet food, though. Just simple stuff. You get 4 out of 5 stars for your guess."

"Thanks for the laughter. I'd probably better go home and get my beauty sleep, though."

Hardly.

"Okay, Brynleigh. Hopefully I'll see you around town. Good luck with the investigation." Why had he ended with that?

With a small smile and a wave, she was gone in her flashy car.

Chapter Five

Monday morning. Brynleigh dug through her closet until she found a suit that might still fit her. Long days at the bookstore called for ripped jeans and funny T-shirts, definitely not boardroom apparel, or her mother's idea of appropriate business attire. Her mother had silk pantsuits in every color with heels to match. This ensemble would have to be good enough.

Parking in the corporation's garage, Brynleigh slipped off her house shoes and slid into the uncomfortable dress shoes. Just being there caused flashbacks of working with her mother before. She had wanted to please her grandfather and had a half-baked idea that, in the process, she might win Celeste's admiration, too. It had not been a fun time, and she suspected it wouldn't be this time around either.

"Miss Brynleigh." Vice President Juliette met her in the lobby.

"Please, just Brynleigh."

"Yes, of course. Let's go upstairs and start some paperwork. Your mother hasn't arrived yet, but she set the meeting for 9am. She should be here any time now." Juliette introduced her to the receptionist and proceeded through the security point.

"Is that really necessary?" Brynleigh whispered as they got on the elevator. Juliette pressed P and turned to her.

"Your mother has a great deal of status in this city and is often hounded by people wanting to save the trees or whatnot. They are often passionate about their cause and want to speak directly to her. More than once, a group has stormed the building, trying to get Ms. Tavish to change the location of whatever project was affecting them personally."

"Oh." Brynleigh knew her mother often rubbed people the wrong way in her not-so-subtle, dollar-encrusted view, but she never considered the possibility of her being in danger. A brief thought about the fire in her bookstore flitted in and just as quickly left as Juliette walked her down to the office suites. "Wow, this is stunning."

"Thanks, it fits my taste." Juliette joined her in front of a large, framed picture. "Lake Como in Italy. My happy place."

"It is beautiful." Chocolate brown furniture with pops of reds and blues matched the color array in the wall hanging. Juliette laid down a novel-sized folder in front of Brynleigh and passed her a pen. "Can I be honest with you for a minute before we start all of this?"

"Of course. I'm not going to be like any other highfalutin executive you've ever worked with."

"Tavish is here. Meeting in five." Vice President Lucas knocked on Juliette's door.

"And especially not like that one." Juliette

whispered behind her hand.

Brynleigh covered a smile with her own hand.

"I'm sorry to hear about your bookstore. I love to read." Juliette closed the folder. "We'll return to this later. Come, our adventures in wonderland begin, Alice."

Brynleigh snickered. "Curiouser and curiouser."

Looked like she'd found a friend.

Juliette straightened her spine and sat down on the luxurious boardroom chair, Brynleigh followed suit. With Lucas across from her and Celeste at the head of the table, the meeting took on the feeling of a royalty court.

"Brynleigh, I trust you have all of the documents you need to proceed in my absence." Celeste started.

A quick glance at Juliette and Brynleigh nodded.

"Speak, child, use your words."

And she was right back to age twelve again. Being chastised for something, unknown to her, but obviously offensive to Celeste.

"Yes, Mother. I will have everything I need to proceed." Brynleigh took a deep breath.

"Lucas, I expect you to show Brynleigh all of the properties and the plans for new projects as soon as possible."

"Yes, ma'am." Lucas sat straight as a board. No slouching for him.

"Okay, bottom line. Everything is run through Brynleigh. She may have been out of this office for a while, but she's smart and she'll catch up. She will be the only one contacting me for anything, is that understood?"

"Yes, ma'am." Lucas and Juliette said in unison.

Celeste talked for another twenty minutes about who-knows-what, and Brynleigh tried to concentrate and take notes. One year, that's all she'd give. Her new bookstore loomed on the horizon, and Brynleigh doodled in the margins of her paper, all the things she could do in the community. Finally, her mother adjourned the meeting and excused herself.

"Looks like we'll be working pretty closely on these projects since I initiated them and fully intend for them to come to fruition." Lucas stood.

"Yes, it does." Brynleigh stood, too.

"Down the rabbit hole we go." Juliette led the way back to her office.

"Well, he hates me." Brynleigh flopped into an oversized swivel chair.

"He thought he was going to be king of the hill." Juliette announced. "He was pretty upset when Celeste told us she was bringing you in."

"'I learned nothing from you except how to be suspicious.'" Brynleigh quipped.

"Ah, To Kill a Mockingbird." Juliette smiled. "'I have a strange feeling with regard to you.'"

"Jane Eyre and I don't think that's in the right context. She's talking to the man in her life."

"Pshaw. It fits, doesn't it?"

"I never wanted to come back here. Or work for my mother again. Did she tell you why she wanted me to step in?"

"Because you're the 'Most Magnificent

Thing?'"

"Ashley Spires."

"'You're all kinds of Wonderful'?"

"Nancy Tillman."

"'It'?"

"Stephen King. And that's not a children's book." Brynleigh grinned. A new friend indeed. "You really don't know why?"

"I know she's sick. But I've never known her to be out. It's got to be serious."

"I'm thinking that way, too."

Note to self- check on how sick Celeste really was and draw up new bookstore plans.

~

Colton pulled out dark dress shoes and held them up to the black pants he had on. They'd have to do. How did one dress as a personal security guard, anyway? Surely, they'll have a uniform for him.

He'd returned the call yesterday to one of his job leads and they'd hired him on the spot. Personal security guard to one of the big wigs at Texas Acquisitions and Development Corporation. Texas A&D was a ginormous company with lots of influential people. He'd had second thoughts about applying for the position without knowing who the personal guard was for, but the salary was the biggest pro. He'd have to clean up his act, best behavior, and all that. He could handle security for just one person, couldn't he? After all, as squad leader, he was responsible for eight men, and he'd been successful up until the last incident. Colton absently rubbed his knee where most of the shrapnel had lodged.

Get your tail in gear.

Colton picked up his backpack, double checked to make sure he had painkillers and water, and left the house. Bandit would not understand his leaving for the entire day without him. Colton hoped he didn't destroy the house in frustration from being cooped up.

The closer he got to the corporation headquarters, the more he tapped his fingers on the steering wheel, turning up the music twice.

What if he hated the individual he was providing security detail for? What if they were a wimpy, sniveling young'un? Or worse yet, a pompous old guy who needed personal attention? Why again had he left the vampire hours and ventured out into the daylight, forcing him to put on a fake smile, fake interest, fake everything? Because of the money. And because it fit his talents perfectly. He was built to lead, but in times of crisis, not in peaceful, civilian settings. Ugh.

Parking in the garage designated for employees, Colton walked into the lobby of the plushest area he'd ever been in. Why was he here again?

"I'm here to see Juliette Romano?" Colton swallowed. This was over the top.

"Of course. Are you Colton Bruens? She said to expect you." The receptionist typed on her keyboard. "She says she'll be right down."

"Thank you." Colton stood off to the side, watching as people filtered through the security point. Apparently, there was a need for security here in the building as well?

"Ah, Mr. Bruens. So good to meet you." The

tall, well-dressed woman approached him.

"Ms. Romano." Colton shook her hand.

"Let's go upstairs and get your creds and badge, then I'll give you a tour."

Colton followed her into the elevator.

The outer doors opened into a waiting area with hallways jutting to either side.

"My office is down this way."

Colton trailed behind, noting the exits and glassed in meeting spaces they passed.

"We are grateful that you are joining us. There's a lot of stir around town about our bigger projects, and your background is perfectly suited to the current needs of the company."

"I understand I'm coming in as personal security for someone. Can you tell me who that's for?"

Juliette stopped at her office doorway. "You mean you don't know who?"

"No." Colton shook his head. "I knew it was a personal detail, but not the actual who."

"Wow. Okay."

Colton backpedaled in his mind. Did he know and had just forgotten? No. Why didn't he ask that question when they'd hired him? What was he walking into? By the look on Juliette's face, he may have made a mistake.

"I'm not entirely comfortable with your reaction to my question." Might as well lay it out there. Upfront.

"Just surprised no one told you."

And that he didn't ask. He heard the unspoken comment, loud and clear.

"The personal detail was for Celeste Tavish, the CEO of the corporation."

What? Wait, *was*?

"Let's see if she's still here." Juliette rose and left the office.

Colton rubbed his chin. Was? He followed her past the elevator and to a set of double doors. He touched her arm before she could open them. "Wait. You said 'was'."

"Things move very fast here, Mr. Bruens." She smiled at him and swung open the doors to a very plush office. Even the carpet was thick and rich-feeling. White couches and white office chairs adorned the suite.

"Mr. Bruens, Celeste Tavish."

Colton shook the offered hand of the CEO of Texas A&D. Her fingers were crowned with diamonds and her palm was soft. The deep buttery color of her pantsuit matched perfectly with her golden hair. Small wrinkles around her mouth moved with her smile which did not quite reach her eyes. This was Celeste Tavish. The CEO of Texas Acquisitions and Development Corporation. Colton blinked and blew out a breath. Wow, he'd really stepped into it now. This was a bigger job than he'd realized. She was known as being sharp, cunning, very wealthy, and a touch cutthroat.

"Welcome, Mr. Bruens." Celeste came around her desk and sat in an office chair beside him. Juliette discreetly left.

Colton sat, as well, stuck on the 'was' comment.

"When we initially put the search out for a

personal security detail for me, there were things going on in the city of Dallas that may not have been conducive to my safety. The board of directors recommended I hire someone who could provide security for me. And so, you were hired. I have it on good reference you were exactly who I needed."

Colton noted all of the past tense words she was using. He sat quietly, listening, but his mind was racing.

"Lucas and I are going out to see the properties. Will you be here when I return?"

Colton and Celeste turned to the voice at the door.

Colton stood up. Brynleigh? What was she doing here?

"What are you doing here?" Brynleigh echoed his thoughts. She looked from Colton to her mother. "What's he doing here?"

"Am I to assume you two know each other somehow?" Celeste moved behind her desk.

"Uh, yes…"

"Not really *know*." Colton started, overlapping her comment.

"Mr. Bruens, my daughter, Brynleigh." Celeste swept her hands at both of them. "Please sit, both of you."

Colton sat back down and watched Brynleigh perch on the edge of the chair Celeste had just vacated. Hesitant to make eye contact with her, he struggled not to flash back to their time outside the burnt bookstore last weekend. Brynleigh adjusted her stance and kept her eyes on her mother. Colton felt the tension rise a notch. What in the world…

"Brynleigh knows this already, but you do not."

Here it comes. Gather intel and then make a decision. Stand down or stay.

"I am taking a leave of absence." Celeste brushed imaginary wrinkles from her slacks. "I have charged Brynleigh with leading the corporation until I return. You will be her personal security until that time."

Colton kept his face still. Brynleigh was his protective assignment? He blinked several times. A mixture of uncomfortable emotions scrolled across his thoughts. No way. Hallelujah. Yep, not happening. Interesting. Walk away. Walk away. No, run.

Brynleigh looked at her hands.

"If you'll excuse me, I must powder my nose." Celeste rose.

Colton assumed that was a pretty term for using the restroom, although the sounds coming from the room Celeste had entered did not sound like powdering. More like, losing her breakfast.

"Sounds like your mom is pretty sick."

"It does sound that way, doesn't it?" Brynleigh stood. "I'd rather not be in here when she comes out. Do you have time to talk? We can use the board room next door."

"Yes, good idea."

"Let me inform Lucas."

Less feminine and more business, the boardroom held a long table, many chairs and a TV at the end.

"Did you know.." They both started.

Colton sat in the chair across from her. She was professional without the closeness he'd imagined Saturday night. Their laughter and bantering were in the past.

"Just so you know, the gala I was at Saturday night with the pretty dress? That's when she laid this on me. I was shocked. And angry."

"Angry I'd be your personal security?" A little offensive.

"No." She started tearing at her cuticles. "Any of it. I knew nothing about you or a personal security detail. She coerced me to go to the gala in the first place and then stood up and announced to the whole world I was taking over the corporation. We'd had one brief conversation and I hadn't given her my answer yet." Brynleigh paused. "One minute I'm loving my bookstore, next thing I know I'm back in the corporate world. My not-happy place. Sorry. This is all a little overwhelming. I don't even know why I need security." She looked across at him. "Do you think this has anything to do with the break in at my store?"

Colton grimaced. That was a huge info dump, one he had few answers to. He found himself moving around the table and sitting in the chair next to her, swiveling it around so their knees almost touched. "I really don't know about all this, but I'm willing to help you figure out if or how everything is connected." Colton resisted the urge to reach out to her. This was quite a puddle he'd stepped into.

"What was your answer going to be?"

"Her leave of absence? I'm pretty sure it's illness related. We both heard how sick she was in the bathroom. It's really more than that, though. This is a family run business, and she wants to make sure it stays that way."

Chapter Six

Later in the day, Brynleigh stood up from behind her mother's obnoxiously large desk. Colton stood, too, from his seat on the couch.

"Ok, look. As nice as it is for there to be someone in the room with me always," Brynleigh coughed into her elbow, "I need to get out for a bit." She smirked. With his good looks and incredibly attractive cologne, she could sit with him in the room for hours, but she was starting to feel caged and overly watched.

"I'll be honest. I'm not exactly sure what or where I'm supposed to be, so you'll have to excuse me if I …"

"Stop." Brynleigh put her hand up. "This is foreign to you, I'm sure. And me? I never wanted to be here again. Let's go get something to eat."

"That is a much better plan."

Brynleigh picked up her jacket and purse. "My car or yours?"

"Have you seen my vehicle?" Colton raised eyebrows at her. "I am not sure you will be comfortable in mine."

"Okay, mine then. You can drive." She tossed

him the keys as she stopped in Juliette's office. Not finding her behind the desk, she stepped next door to Lucas' office. She had yet to be in here, and she found the dark heavy wood replicated her mother's office. Interesting. "Lucas, I'm going out for a bit."

Vice President Lucas met her at the door. "Do you need company?" His gaze flicked to Colton standing near the elevator.

"No, Mr. Bruens will be with me. We'll be back soon."

"When you return, I'll take you to see the properties. Your mother's insistence."

Clearly not a request, and Lucas seemed less than thrilled to fulfill the expectation.

"Yes, of course."

Once in the elevator, Brynleigh swiped her ID over the keypad, and pushed the appropriate button and turned to Colton.

"Not sure how I feel about that one."

"Lucas?"

"Yes."

"So noted."

Brynleigh liked the way he took her words and appeared to care about what she said. Conversations with her mother were generally one-sided, and any comment she did have was brushed to the side as frivolous.

"This is where the executives park?"

Brynleigh led him to her car. "You haven't been here yet?"

"No. I've walked the building, found all the exits and blind spots, but didn't realize there was a separate parking garage."

"It takes a special badge ID to get here."

Colton nodded his head, unlocked the car, and opened her door.

Brynleigh was unprepared for how much room his shoulders took up and how close the bucket seats forced them to be. She inhaled his cologne and smiled inwardly. Yum.

"This is nice." Colton pushed the start button and the car roared to life.

"I like her. I call her Carly." Brynleigh patted the dashboard and tried not to notice how strong his hands looked on the steering wheel.

"Where are we heading?"

"I know a little bistro just on the edge of town. They serve amazing sandwiches."

"Betty Sue's?"

"Yes. How do you know about Betty Sue's?"

"Used to grab a chocolate handheld pie for a midnight snack on my shifts at the village."

"Nice. Those strawberry rhubarb ones are good, too."

~

"Thank you, but you really should've let me pay for lunch." Brynleigh picked up paper sandwich linings in plastic red diner bowls littering the table. The waitress came by and refilled her frosty mug of root beer and his large, iced tea. "Were you expecting a Die Hard scenario when you hired on?"

Brynleigh's question came out of the blue after their lunch small talk.

"Die Hard? You think I look like Bruce Willis?"

Brynleigh shook her head. "Not look like him,

although…" She paused.

He dared her with his eyes to finish that sentence. "Although what?"

"Nothing." She turned pink under his scrutiny. "I never knew my mother needed protection. I've never needed protection. And from what? And why don't I have protection at home? Just the office."

Valid questions. Colton had thought the same thing. Why only at the office? Did Celeste Tavish have a bodyguard at home?

"Are you asking me to come home with you?" Did that just come out of his mouth? That kind of humor would get him booted off the job. It was interesting to see her turn a darker shade of pink, though. "Just kidding. I asked myself the same questions. About Celeste." Neutral territory. Come on, dude, get it together. She was making his hormones and self-control work overtime.

"A little bold, aren't you? But seriously, how concerned should I be?"

"I don't know yet. Let's keep our eyes open. Are you willing to share intel with me if you uncover anything important?"

"Intel?"

"Sorry, habit. Anything noteworthy or gut reaction."

"Of course." Brynleigh gathered their trash and dumped it in the receptacle. "We should probably head back. I'm still looking at all those projects Mother was in the middle of."

Colton followed her out to the car. "Stop."

Instant fear crossed her face.

"Oh sorry." Colton opened the door for her and

then settled into the driver's seat. "I will always open the door for you. It's called respect."

"And I was going to beat you to the car… I get it."

"Good to know you follow directions well." Colton patted her hand and then shook his head. Why could his brain and his mouth not line up? Saying the dumbest things and flirting with her, things totally out of his character. And yet, she was alluring and comfortable drawing him out. He thought of her often. Thought about how to protect her. Where she might go, blind spots along the way. Where she might like to go for dinner…Good grief.

~

Brynleigh laughed to herself when she thought about lunch and how uncomfortable Colton had been with her. He was fun and made her laugh one minute and then on guard and aloof the next. She loved his chivalrous and protective attitude. She bet he had been a great leader in the military. She could sense the darkness around the edges, though, as if there were ugly things in his past. Maybe in a different setting, they could've become friends or maybe more. Brynleigh let her mind wander on what the "more" might look like. Was he moody? A closet romantic? Would he treat her like he did his mother? He never mentioned family in the short time they'd spent together.

"You're back. Ready to go look at some properties?" Lucas stood in her doorway.

Brynleigh carefully put away her thoughts with the hopes of pulling them back out later.

"I am."

Lucas was down by the elevator by the time she walked out of her office.

"Going to look at properties with Lucas." Brynleigh called to Juliette. She was on the phone and gave her a thumb's up sign. Colton had his head down, looking at paperwork on the round table in Juliette's office, but stood when she stepped in.

"Do you want me to go with you?"

Very tempting offer.

"No. I think I'll be safe with a Vice President."

Colton pursed his lips, clearly not convinced, but didn't comment.

"You don't have to announce where you're going every single time you leave the office." Lucas tossed over his shoulder, entering the elevator.

Brynleigh frowned at him. He was going to take getting used to, and vice versa. "I find it's respectful to let people know you're out of the office."

"You're the acting CEO. It's nobody's business."

Note to self, this guy did not like her much. Which is probably why he got along with Mother.

Lucas walked up to a luxury car and clicked his fob. Not waiting for her, or opening her door for her, he slid into the driver's seat.

"Okay." Second note to self. Lucas was not chivalrous at all.

"We've got several places to see…"

The tone of his voice was putting her to sleep, fast, as he rattled on and on. Third note to self, there were a lot of 'I's' in those statements, instead of Texas A&D. Gathering … what did Colton call it?

Gathering intel. The file was going to be large, and insignificant, when she got back to Colton. Would he have left the building by the time they returned?

"Are you listening?" Lucas tapped his hand on the steering wheel.

"I am. Go ahead."

"This next property is coming along nicely. We've got acreage to the east I'm confident he will sell to me. If not, I may have to resort to legal means. I'm hoping it won't come to that, though. Would really cut into my profits."

"Tell me again your vision for this property?" Brynleigh stepped out of the car. She could see a variety of outbuildings, what looked to be a main road, and several cattle pens. "No one lives here?"

"It wouldn't matter if they did. No, not in this area. Over there, is a ranch, I think, that has juveniles living there, but I don't think it's zoned right to run a business legally. And just past those trees is a working cattle ranch which shouldn't interfere with what we're going to do. Again, they're just peons scratching out an existence; shouldn't put up much of a fight." Lucas pointed to the west.

"Would you bulldoze the little town down?" It was clearly vacant.

"We'd build it up, glamorize it, make it into the most glittery western town you've ever seen. It wouldn't be recognizable when we were done with it."

"And who owns it now?" Brynleigh could see dollar signs in Lucas' eyes.

"Some old man. They do something called Cowboy Action Shooting at the town site. They'll be grateful for the cash we throw their way for the property."

"Hmmm…" Lucas' attitude was arrogant and boastful. Unlike Colton.

"I'll show you the ranch and then the other areas we are progressing on." Lucas started the car.

As they drove south past the cattle ranch, Brynleigh noted the large wooden sign, "Rodeo This Weekend". Maybe she'd stop in and see for herself what the landowners were like.

Lucas informed her he was done for the day and dropped Brynleigh off at the front doors of the corp building. She noticed Juliette's light was still on.

"Are you going home any time soon?" She startled Juliette. "Oh, sorry, I thought you heard me clunking down the hall."

"Yes, I just wanted to finish this one report. How was your ride with Lucas?"

Brynleigh hesitated. "Enlightening." She didn't know Juliette well enough to be candid, despite suspecting that she could be.

"Enlightening as in it's nice to see the projects Texas A&D is involved in or enlightening as in Lucas?"

"As in Lucas."

"You seem like a very smart person. I would be very observant."

Brynleigh came farther in the room. "Something I should know?"

Juliette shrugged.

"Seriously, if I should be aware of something, please give me a heads up."

"There are things I'd go about differently."

Brynleigh lifted her eyes to the ceiling. There was that uncomfortable feeling she had in the pit of her stomach again. The same one she had when Lucas was talking about "any means necessary" to get what he…the corporation…wanted. "Like what?"

"Let's pick this up tomorrow, shall we? It's getting late and you've had a big day."

"Fine, but let me end with this. My whole purpose in life is to make things better for the people around me and the community so if this corporation isn't about that or Lucas has his own ideas, you may see some shaking going on."

"Lean on Me." Juliette smiled. "If you need to."

"Song. Bill Withers. Not a book title." Brynleigh waved and left her office.

Chapter Seven

"Hey, I know you just got home, but I was wondering if you could drive some cattle over to the ranch next door tonight?" His brother sat down next to Colton on the picnic bench. "They've got the rodeo tomorrow night."

"They're using our cattle for the rodeo? What have you got going on?" Colton asked.

"Yep. And the goats. I'm herding them over since you seem to be allergic to them."

Colton rolled his eyes. Mark wasn't wrong though, he wanted nothing to do with the goats.

"You can take Billy and one of the others with you."

Billy made eye contact with Colton from his spot in the yard. Great, the kid had probably heard his conversation about the goats.

"We'll go over first. Don't want to eat your dust." Colton stood. "Are they ready for us now?"

"I'll call ahead."

Colton hollered at Billy, motioned to one of the other boys he didn't know and went to saddle his horse.

"You ever ridden before?" Colton threw a saddle up on a tall bay for the younger boy.

"I don't need your help." Billy spat on the ground and drug a saddle over to a calm gray mare.

Colton watched him struggle. Clearly, he did need help. Quietly, he came up behind Billy and pulled the saddle out of his hands. He could see the frustrated tears in the boy's eyes, but didn't acknowledge them. To do so would only hurt his pride more.

"We're just going to do a slow herd." Colton pointed at the tall kid. "You, go get in the back and gently walk behind. Billy, you take the right side and I'll get the left. Stay even with me. We'll point them down the lane and go until the cowboys up ahead can take them."

"Why can't you just load them in a trailer?" Billy grumbled.

"We may do that on the way back. This is easier and it's just down the road."

"Sounds like a lot of work."

"Which you're opposed to?"

Billy rolled his eyes.

"I'd rather be on the back of a horse than sitting starin' at nothing."

The boys did exactly what he instructed, and Colton began to relax in the saddle. After ten minutes, the other ranch cowboys came into view and gathered off to the side of the lane.

"We'll let them pass and then take them from here," the cowboy on the big Appaloosa called. Once past, the other cowboys joined with him and the boys.

"If it's all the same to you, we'll ride up there with you."

"Sure. Name's Paul." The cowboy took off his glove and leaned across the saddle to shake Colton's hand.

"Colton. These boys need to finish what they started. Good for them."

"They seem to be doing great."

Colton nodded. He noticed the younger boy nodding off to the soothing motion as his horse plodded along behind the herd.

Once in the pen, he let the boys get off their horses and sit on the bench for a minute. Inexperienced saddle riders, they'd be sore in the back end by morning. Shoot, he'd be sore, too.

"Can I interest you in some lemonade?" A pretty woman stood on the porch, holding a glass pitcher.

"Yes. I'm Colton Bruens from the next ranch over." He offered her his hand.

"I remember you, Colton Bruens, just barely. You were a little older than me in school."

"Hmm…sorry, I didn't really pay attention to anyone younger than me."

"You were well known in my class. The pitcher for the baseball team. All of the girls swooned over you."

"Those were the days." Colton reached out to the man who came to stand by her on the porch. "Colton."

"Brandon."

"Just delivering the cattle for the rodeo. My brother's following with the goats." His comment dripped with disgust.

Brandon laughed. "Can you come in for a cup

of coffee?"

Colton looked at the glass of lemonade in his hand. "Billy, come here. You take this and see if this nice lady has a glass for the other boy. I've got a little time until Mark gets here."

"Cool." Brandon led him to a large wooden table near the kitchen. Colorful rugs added dimension to the warm southwest colors.

Colton accepted the cup of coffee. "Are you the ranch owner?"

"No. My wife, Selena's father, is the foreman."

"Ah, I wasn't sure."

"I'm a transplant. Selena and I met. I fell in love with her, but she wanted nothing to do with me. I convinced her I was the best man for her, and she still hated me. Just kidding. About the hate part. We got married about six months ago."

"Congratulations."

"Thanks. Have you always lived at the ranch next door?"

"My family has. I joined the military and left for a bit." Colton clenched his jaw.

Selena came inside, and Colton watched her and Brandon share a glance. It was warm and sweet and made him feel like an outsider. An intruder looking in on an intimate moment. Someday he'd have that. A hopeful pipe dream. In all honesty, would anyone want him after they got to know him a little? Or his family history? He would not repeat that with anyone.

"You should come out to the rodeo tomorrow night."

"Yeah, I might."

"It's Faith and Family night."

"What does that mean?"

"We'll have kiddy games set up, and we have a Christian country singer putting on a mini concert after the bull riding."

"We'll see. Thanks for the invite." Might be kinda fun. He wasn't interested in the family part or the Christian concert, but the rest of it would be entertaining.

"You said you were in the military? Me, too. Semper Fi."

"Yeah, not that one. Army." Colton grinned.

"When were you in?"

"Just finished my second tour in Afghanistan." Colton took his hand away from his knee. Too late. Brandon missed little. "Brought a little back with me."

"Shrapnel still in there?"

"Nah, they got it all, but it sure hurts sometimes."

"I understand." Brandon pulled up his shirt sleeve.

Colton whistled. Underneath the eagle tattoo, the ragged edge of a knife wound protruded. "That's a little close."

"Heard them coming. Had a little surprise waiting." Brandon lightly punched Colton. "But, by the grace of God, I got outta there."

"Me, too, although I'm pretty sure my men had more to do with it than God."

Brandon looked at him long and hard.

God, and Brynleigh, were certain to invade his sleep tonight.

Chapter Eight

"Good morning." Brynleigh pushed the phone farther up on her shoulder as she fixed her coffee.

"Good morning to you, too. It's Friday." Juliette sing-songed.

"And Sunday's coming."

"What?"

"Sorry, it's a book title. I thought we were talking in book titles again." Brynleigh loved this exchange with Juliette. "Hey, I'll be a little late today. I want to check out property without my bodyguard or Lucas."

"Okay. Mr. Bruens might not be too happy."

"He'll get over it."

"He is very handsome in a rugged kind of way."

"Juliette-"

"I know, I know. I'll stay in my lane."

"I'll be in around noon hopefully."

"Okay, sure. See you then."

Lucas may not feel she needed to check in, but that fell under the category of good work ethic for her.

Brynleigh had an idea in the middle of the night to look into the two ranches affected by the new casino Texas A&D wanted built. She was certain she could locate them even though Lucas had been driving and she hadn't been paying attention to directions as close as she could have been. West of the city and a little south, she came upon a smaller two-lane highway that looked familiar. Turning down a lane surrounded on either side by cattle fencing, she drove up to the first ranch easily.

This was the one that owned the western town used for shooting competitions, she reminded herself. She hoped her arrival wasn't too early.

"Hello?"

Brynleigh startled when a cowboy called to her outside her car. Getting out, she offered her hand. "Brynleigh Tavish, are you the owner of the ranch?"

The man smiled at her under the wide sombrero. "No, ma'am. Would you like me to get him for you?"

"Yes, please."

"Papa?" A woman her age came from an outbuilding, holding the edge of her apron.

The man smiled again, bowed, and turned away.

Was this the owner? He'd said 'him' so Brynleigh assumed this wasn't the owner either.

"Hi, I'm Brynleigh Tavish."

"I'd shake your hand, but then I'd probably drop all of the girls' hard work." The woman opened her apron to show Brynleigh all of the eggs she had gathered this morning.

"Oh sure. Listen, I hope I'm not too early. I just

wanted to-"

"Come on in. We can talk inside. And I know who you are."

Wow, news traveled fast.

Brynleigh watched as the woman rinsed the eggs and placed them gently in the fridge. Wiping her hand on a kitchen towel, she reached out to Brynleigh as if to hug her.

Oh, okay. Pretty informal. Hugs versus handshakes.

"Selena Sollor. I am so sorry to hear about your bookstore."

Oh, surprise. Again.

"How did you hear about my bookstore?"

"I went there a lot."

"Yes, I remember you now. You were always looking for travel books. Did you go on a grand vacation?" Now it was starting to make sense. She did remember Selena.

"The vacation of a lifetime. I got married." Selena poured coffee into a carafe and set it on the table between them. Two sturdy mugs, sugar, and napkins were plopped down next to the carafe. "I'm assuming you drink coffee? How do you take it?"

"Oh, please. None for me. I take way too much creamer in mine to have coffee out in public."

"Nonsense. I like a little coffee with my creamer, too." Selena jumped up and grabbed a gallon sized creamer container out of the fridge. "See?"

"Then I will have some." Brynleigh warmed to Selena's hospitality. "And congratulations."

"Thanks. He exceeds my every dream and

expectation."

"Wow, he must be quite a guy." Colton's face popped in her mind. He was physically dreamy, for sure, with his wide shoulders and strong arms. But her dream man? She didn't really know him except for his examples of being kind and gentlemanly with a great sense of humor.

"I was referring to God, but Brandon is pretty great, too." Selena snickered.

"Oh sorry, I just assumed…"

"No problem. I just never expected someone like Brandon, and God orchestrated every piece of the journey. Now, that's a story for another time. What can I help you with?"

That was a story she'd like to hear. Brynleigh knew there was a God, but how could he orchestrate anything? Her mother could. Was God like her mother? A manipulative mastermind?

She blew out a breath. What she had to say may change the whole tone of the visit.

"I already told you my name. Ever since my store burned down, and with extenuating circumstances, I've found myself back in the corporate world working for Texas A&D. Does that ring a bell?"

"It does." Selena sipped her coffee.

"Maybe I should be speaking to the owner of the ranch."

"He's away right now. I run the ranch, along with my husband, when he's away."

"I see. If you're familiar with Texas A&D, you know they are planning to buy the western town north of here under this ranch's name." Brynleigh studied her for a reaction.

"And our neighbor's ranch."

"Yes, I'm heading there next."

"You said 'they', not 'we'. What can we do for you?"

"I wanted to get to know the owners. I have a gut feeling about all of this and I wanted to at least meet you."

"Before you buy our land and build an awful casino in its place?"

"If you frequented my bookstore, you saw all of the community activities I lined up each month. It would never be my intention to tear down something that also benefited the community."

"So, you're on a fact-finding mission." Selena relaxed against the table. "I know casinos bring in money and little operations like ours and our neighbors don't seem significant. I'd encourage you to investigate a little further. We both are involved in our communities."

"I will. I'm not sold on this being the best investment. Which is why the 'they' and not 'we'." Brynleigh smiled at her.

"Got it. Did they ever find out what caused the fire at the bookstore?"

Brynleigh searched Selena's face. She had not heard from the police or the fire department about the investigation. Note to self, call and check. She'd been so busy with Texas A&D, she'd let that slip off her radar. "No, not yet."

"Were you able to save the huge metal warrior that stood in the corner?"

"The tin man? That's what I called him."

"Yes, the tin man. It's actually a Roman soldier like from Bible times. I always admired it when I came in. Can you imagine wearing all of the armor in battle? I like to think about that when I'm studying my Bible."

Interesting. Brynleigh didn't know what she was talking about, but Selena was excited. "Do you want it? I pulled it out the next day and cleaned it up. It's not damaged. It scares the daylights out of me after I've turned out the lights."

"Yes, I want it. That's awesome." Selena laid her hand on Brynleigh's arm. "Why don't you come out to the rodeo tomorrow night? It's here and not at the western town. I can introduce you to some more folks."

"I may. I'll have to borrow a truck from someone to get the tin man to you. He won't fit in my car. I tried."

"Oh sure. Or I can send someone to you. We'll figure it out." Selena stood when Brynleigh did.

"I should probably go. I want to stop by the other ranch, too."

"Want me to call ahead so someone can meet you at the gate? The perimeter is monitored with cameras and an alarm system."

"Why the security?"

"Mark, the owner of the ranch, runs a boys ranch on the property."

"I don't know what that means."

"There are boys who have gotten into trouble and the court system sends them to Mark first instead of juvenile jail, especially if they don't have family or their family situation isn't stable. Mark's got quite a thing going, if you ask me. It's also a working cattle ranch, and where we get our rodeo supply from, and everyone who lives there has responsibilities. Mark is a great guy."

And Texas A&D only sees dollar signs. Lucas, if he cared, probably did not know how valuable the ranch's services were to the community.

"Yes, if you would, that would be great."

"Hopefully, we'll see you tomorrow?"

"I think so. Thanks for the invite."

Brynleigh got in her car and drove back up the dusty lane. Lucas had been passionate about the casino. She was not.

~

"What do you mean, she went out on her own?" Colton stood in Juliette's doorway, arms on the door frame.

Juliette raised her eyebrows. "Would you like to come in or do you want to stand there, bellowing at me?"

"Sorry." Colton folded into a leather chair opposite Juliette's desk. Thoughts of the bookstore fire raced through his head. She'd called 911 that night. She now had a security detail on her at work. Why hadn't he put something in place at her home? They were both green to their positions and so far, nothing indicated she was in danger from anything other than her mother's harsh words and Vice President Lucas' surly personality. "Do you know where she went? Or when she'll be back?"

"She said by early afternoon, hopefully."

Colton groaned. "Well, I guess, I'll wander the building until she gets back. This is my number if you need me."

"I'm sure I already have it, being the vice president over HR…"

"Sorry, I'll leave it for you so you don't have to look it up." Colton left her office after writing his cell number on a slip of paper. Passing Lucas' office, his eyes met Lucas' briefly. He was sure Lucas had heard the whole exchange with Juliette.

~

Brynleigh pulled up to the wrought iron gate and pushed the intercom button. After a second, the gate swung open, and she bumped across the cattle guard buried in the dirt. She passed a two-story house and proceeded on to the low ranch building with a blue truck sitting out front. A man came off the porch, his baseball hat shielding his eyes.

"Good morning. I'm Mark."

Brynleigh got out of her car, admiring the clean property complete with wildflowers in watering cans on the steps. A female touch, although Selena had only mentioned Mark.

"Brynleigh Tavish."

"Nice to meet you." Mark invited her onto the porch and into one of the comfy chairs.

"Just wanted to stop in and visit with you for a bit. I'm sure Selena told you what I'm doing."

"She did. She speaks very highly of you."

Selena didn't even know her, except through the bookstore. There had been a comfortable, almost familiar, nature to their conversation, but still…

"That's nice of her to say."

"What can I do for you? Show you around? Selena said she told you about the boys, who we may encounter. And then, they may all stay hidden, scared to talk to a pretty woman such as yourself."

Brynleigh blushed. "I'd love to see what you do here."

Mark explained the court system arrangement, the number of boys housed at the ranch, and the expectations he had for each of them. "This isn't jail, although they may act like it is. They can run away, but the security cameras would notify us. That would cost them dearly, though, in the eyes of the court."

"Why the gate at the end of the driveway, then?"

"It's got a motion detector camera on it, and is basically for those coming in, not keeping the boys in. We, occasionally, have an unauthorized parent who wants to visit their boy. It really just lets us know someone's coming down the lane."

Mark and Brynleigh walked down to the barn.

"This is where we house the goats." He pulled a heavy barn door open and immediately three goats fell over, legs quivering in the air.

"Oh my goodness, what happened?" Brynleigh cried out.

"They're fainting goats. I opened the door too quickly and didn't announce our presence appropriately."

Brynleigh laughed as one-by-one the little goats shook off their coats and stood. Going back to what they were doing prior to the door opening, they ran off and jumped from hay bale to hay bale.

"Look at them jump." She'd watched goats play on videos, but never in real life. They were hysterical. She couldn't contain her laughter as the phrase 'jump for joy' crossed her mind. They were such fun to watch.

"We have cattle and horses, too, and each boy has certain responsibilities as well as daily school instruction and normal living expectations."

"Who teaches them?" Brynleigh thought about the computers and readers that were burned up in the fire. She missed the interaction with the kids in the community who would come to her for extra help or a tutoring session.

"I do, for now. I have a teaching degree, and an undergraduate degree in social work. My real love is teaching them through the Bible. I don't have a degree in theology, just experience."

First Selena, and now Mark.

"And they each have a case manager who checks on their progress. We do good work here with the boys. I know a casino will be advantageous to Texas A&D. Please consider what we do is just as advantageous to the community."

"I will." Brynleigh's heart broke at the thought of kicking these people off their property. Maybe there was another way. Based on Lucas' excitement and determination, it would be an uphill climb.

Colton was waiting for her in the office lobby when she returned. His clenched jaw and hard stare followed her as she slipped off the elevator. "Where have you been?"

After a cool look, she stepped up to him. "I might remind you I am the acting CEO and you answer to me. Not the other way around. I might also remind you I don't have your cell number. And thirdly, we talked about not needing a security detail while I'm not at work." Brynleigh walked down to her office, Colton following.

"It is office hours," he retorted.

Brynleigh cocked her head and pinched her lips together. He was acting like a sulky kid. He left the office in silence after flinging down a piece of paper with his cell number scratched on it. She didn't see him again until the end of the day when he nodded at her from the security point in the building lobby.

Chapter Nine

"**Don't you want** to get out for a while, go to the rodeo, see something you've never seen before?" Mark looked exasperated.

Colton walked past as Mark and Billy squared off in the hallway. He was ready for something different. He didn't really care if the boy wasn't, but he'd back up his brother. If the kid didn't go, someone would have to hang back with him and make sure he didn't blow up the place.

"Those cattle we ran over there last night will see some action. Don't you want to see them?" Colton ventured, walking around them, fastening the remainder of his shirt snaps.

"What do I care about ugly cows?"

Colton started to correct him. They weren't cows, they were heifers.

"You'll get to see your goats," Billy whispered.

Colton lunged at the kid. Mark jumped in front of him, blocking his view. Toe to toe, they were even height, although Colton had more muscle than Mark on his side.

"Colt-" Mark put his hand on Colton's chest. "Slow it down. He's just a kid."

"A kid who needs a lesson on when to keep his mouth shut." Colton spun on his heel and headed the opposite direction. He'd almost lost it. Lost control. Over a stupid comment, by a stupid kid. He scratched his forehead. He could usually ignore sarcasm, dismiss it the same as he wrapped up the pickles he hadn't ordered on his sandwich and toss them all in the trash. He was edgy tonight. His emotions were raw and sitting on his chest right below his mouth, itching to explode. Why? Probably because of Brynleigh's stubborn excuse to call in late and not tell him where she was going. He didn't have any responsibility for her outside of work, they'd talked about that. It was a workday, however, and she'd gone off without him. Left him sitting on his hands, pestering Juliette, and wondering what he was supposed to be doing.

Brynleigh. And God. Both kept coming up. What if there was a God like Brandon mentioned? One who showed up when a person was in trouble? God hadn't shown up when he was growing up. His mother put her faith in God and look how it turned out for her. She survived his father, but succumbed to cancer. Where was God in that mess? Colton had heard her crying and praying on more than one occasion in her bedroom, but never once did he see God intervene. The God she spoke about was a Savior, but He'd failed to save her. Not in Colton's teenage eyes. At one point, he'd come home from baseball practice to find Mark bandaging up his mother, blood dripping from a split lip. His father had already left the house and his mother refused to go to the hospital or call the cops. Colton stayed up that night, drank half a stolen bottle of whiskey from the liquor cabinet, and waited for his father to come home. Luckily, his father hadn't come home for weeks and only when Colton was gone to a baseball tournament, did he return to the house. Hot and tired, Colton had entered the house, ready to fight, and found his mother had forgiven his father and everything was right in the world again.

Colton snorted. Right in the world. Never again.

Maybe God was only for the good people.

He should get on a bull tonight, release some negativity. Colton snorted again. He'd never been on a bull. He'd get himself killed. And then where would Miss Brynleigh be? Without security, which is what she apparently preferred based on her antics earlier.

~

This should be fun. Brynleigh laced up her boots and tucked her shirt into her jeans. It had been a long time since she'd been to a rodeo. Dallas was as Texas as they came, but the glitzy, everything's-bigger-than, Texas. Not a dusty, little side town. The city itself was encroaching on those towns, expanding the glitter and taking over the hometown feel with big city lights. And the reason why those two ranches were in the path of expansion.

She wouldn't think about that tonight. Tonight was free from stress. A night out. Brynleigh looked forward to seeing Selena again. She and Brandon were cute together. Maybe spending more time with them would ease the loss in her personal life and the closed down, burnt bookstore. Maybe God was opening a new door for her like Juliette had mentioned when Brynleigh expressed how much she missed her community and serving with the kids. Why would He, though?

Brynleigh tapped on the Tin Man's chest as she walked by.

"You may be getting a new home, mister."

She smiled. She definitely needed a night out if she was going to continue talking to a tall, metal guy. The fact he didn't talk back was a plus, but he'd already scared her multiple times and she was ready for him to go bye-bye.

Colton Bruens was a different story. She probably should have told him she'd be in late. After all, he was assigned to her at work. She grimaced. She wasn't used to letting everyone in on her decisions. He probably felt like she wasn't letting him do his job, but in truthfulness, she hadn't thought about letting anyone else know except Juliette. Brynleigh pulled her hair up and French braided it, leaving tendrils around her face. A little lip gloss and she was ready to go.

~

Colton pushed his way through the bundle of people and sat down near the end of the arena so he could see the chutes. Most of the action would happen on the other end, if the crowd was lucky, but he wanted to see how the cattle they brought over performed out of the gate.

Mark had been forced to stay home since Billy was acting out. That was just fine with Colton.

The heifers were bawling, and dust flew as the pens were readied for the rodeo. The announcer greeted the crowd and introduced the pickup cowboys already in the arena as well as the rodeo clowns.

"Folks, please stand for the national anthem," the announcer boomed.

Colton stood, took his hat off, and listened to the young girl sing the song that opened every sporting event, rodeo included. He noticed a young guy in front of him stay seated, obnoxiously sucking on a drink. Colton's temperature went up. People like this guy knew nothing of patriotism, service, or sacrifice. He'd never experienced the lack of freedom in war torn countries. Colton wanted to hit him, knock him out cold. His fists clenched with restraint.

"You need to stand up, buddy." Colton shouted at him.

"You talkin' to me? I ain't got to do anything. Mind your own business."

"I did mind mine, and yours, too, while you were over here in the US of A acting like a baby." Colton called back at him.

The man flipped him the finger. The song ended with applause from the crowd. Colton sat down and tried to concentrate on the rodeo. The man's disrespect stuck in his craw.

Colton's heart rate slowed down as he watched his favorite rodeo event, team roping. There was something about working as a team to accomplish a goal that was so rewarding. He thought about his military teammates. If the results of the team working together were positive, everyone went home happy. If the ending was not the desired outcome, a person could find themselves state-side with an injured canine partner. Colton shook off the thoughts that led down a dark road. Tonight was all about fun.

Colton watched a pretty blond walk by holding a tray of nachos in one hand and a bucket of beer bottles in the other. He could use one of those which would not be wise with every fiber of his being teetering over a black abyss. The lady passed by him, and he could smell the jalapenos and cheesy cheese. Making her way carefully to the stands, she stopped by the jerk Colton had engaged with earlier during the national anthem. As she offered the plate of nachos to him, the man slapped them out of her hand and grabbed for the bucket of beer. The lady looked around to see if anyone else had seen the exchange and tears coursed down her cheeks.

Colton came unglued at the look on the lady's face. Roaring down the steps, Colton rammed his fist into the man's ear, toppling him to the ground. The lady screamed. Colton was too far in the red zone to stop now. He pummeled him repeatedly. Bucking him off, the man jumped up and swung at Colton, busting open his nose. Blood gushed down his face. With his head ringing, Colton felt his body being pulled off the man.

"Take him up to the house. I know him. You can get statements from them first," a voice said, behind Colton.

The cops led him up to a small house used as a first aid station. He grabbed a towel from a nearby counter and mopped the blood from his face. His T-shirt was effectively ruined, tattered and blood-stained. Based on the feel of the split on his nose, he would probably have black eyes, complete in time for his second week of work. Colton blew out a breath and took off his shirt, attempting to get the blood out. Knowing the mood he had been in all day, he should never have ventured out into public. His fists and his thoughts got away from him, and he'd let the demons out.

Colton looked up to see Brandon standing over him, quiet.

He didn't even know Brandon, having only just met him when they brought the cattle over. Colton looked back down at his hands, rough and scratched. His muscles quivered in the aftermath of the anger that had consumed him. Sniffing blood up his nose and down his throat, Colton leaned over and spit in the sink. Thankfully, it wasn't deep red which meant it was slowing down and coagulating as it should.

"Want to tell me what happened?" Brandon folded his arms and blocked Colton's view of the cops.

Not really. Colton spit again and mopped a droplet of blood off his bare chest with the now-ruined shirt. However, it appeared Brandon may be his chance to not go to jail tonight.

He shrugged. "I let that idiot get to me. He ignored the national anthem and then slapped the nachos out of that poor girl's hands. I just couldn't let it go."

"Colton, you are a soldier. You know you can't go around using your fists."

He shook his head, refusing to make eye contact. No, he wasn't. Not anymore. He was more like his father than he wanted to believe.

"Colton. Look at me."

Slowly, every muscle groaning, Colton stood. He pulled his arm up in a salute.

"Really?" Brandon sighed. "I'm not your superior, nor am I military, so I assume this is your way of sticking it to me? Sit down."

Colton dropped back into the chair.

"I am going to yell at you as if I were, though." Brandon started shouting. "You sport those tattoos as signs you're a soldier and yet, you do dumb things like this? Why should I not let you go to jail? Huh? Why, soldier?"

"I deserve it."

"Oh, really? That's your excuse?" Brandon continued to yell.

"Look, I didn't mean to disrespect you. I don't want to go to jail."

"Colton, I've known you for all of twenty-four hours, and I don't know what happened 'cuz I wasn't there. But, I really don't think this is who you are. Call it a gut feeling or whatever, but tell me I'm wrong."

Colton pressed his lips together and looked at everything, but Brandon.

Brandon slapped his bicep tattoo. Colton flinched. "You're a warrior, bro, start acting like one."

The outer door flew open, banging against the wall. Both Colton and Brandon looked up.

Brynleigh burst into the room. "Oh my... what happened?"

Chapter Ten

Brynleigh looked at Colton, shirtless, and with blood on his face. Brandon stood over him. She'd seen the skirmish, but didn't realize it was Colton until the policemen were walking him up the hill.

Brandon threw Colton a hooded sweatshirt from the closet, and Brynleigh watched as he struggled to cover himself.

"I don't know what happened out there," Brynleigh pointed a finger at the rodeo grounds, "but I will see you in my office first thing on Monday."

"I'm not on duty."

"Your actions outside of Texas A&D affect how you are perceived on duty. Especially if you're head of security AND a hothead."

"Yes, ma'am."

Brynleigh stormed out and down to her car. The rodeo was still going on, however, she was done for the evening. Clearly, Colton had no self-control, and was too much drama for her. She needed peaceful people around her, not ones who jumped at a fight. What in the world had set him off? Wonder what the other guy looked like? She'd ask Selena later if

Brandon knew anything more. Colton better not go to jail. He couldn't serve as security from there. Maybe a night wouldn't hurt him, though.

Brynleigh's thoughts drifted to the sight of him without his shirt. He was toned and muscular, but not like weightlifters with veins bulging out. The sight of his bloody face had nearly undone her. He was nice to look at, even with the split nose.

But, the drama? He was high-strung in a controlled way, arrogant, broody, and unpredictable. He alluded to a dark history and those demons who peeked out occasionally. Her mother generated enough drama.

Brynleigh pulled into her driveway and opened the garage door by remote. Glass glinted off the paved way to her front steps.

"What in the world?"

She stepped closer to the glass shards and realized her bay window had a hole the size of her head in the center of it. Cracks splintered through the rest of the glass. The outer glass on the two-paned window was shattered on the front lawn. She could only imagine what her front room must look like.

Entering through the garage, she paused in the mudroom doorway and surveyed the damage to her house. A brick lay in the middle of the floor, the obvious culprit. Brynleigh tip-toed through the glass and looked closer at the brick. LEAVE in heavy block letters was spray painted on one side. Leave? Leave what? Her home?

Brynleigh called 911 and reported the vandalism. Her throat constricted as she answered the police dispatcher's questions. Yes, she was in the home. Yes, she could see what damaged the window. Did she think she was safe? Brynleigh looked around. She hadn't thought about anyone being in the house. The alarm company would have called her if any of the doors had been breached. Yes, she believed she was safe. The police would be out to take a statement shortly, in the meantime, don't touch anything.

Brynleigh sat and rested her head on the kitchen table. This night was not getting any better. The noises in the house, normal settling noises, did not feel normal, and she sat still and watched the tree out front, dancing in the light cast from the moon. A light breeze blew in through the hole. Brynleigh shivered. She did not feel safe like she'd told the dispatcher. Anything could come through that hole. And the message on the brick was clearly intended to scare her, but from what she had no idea.

She pulled out the paper with Colton's phone number on it. If he wasn't in jail, he would help her. Despite her angry retort about his off-duty behavior, she could use his protective attitude right now.

"Colton?"

He picked up on the first ring.

"Are you in jail?" She realized how stupid that sounded. If he were in jail, he couldn't answer his phone. "Colton?"

He sighed, heavily, into the phone. "Brynleigh, I'm really sorry about-"

Brynleigh cut him off. "Someone threw a rock in my window, and it shattered everywhere."

"Wait, what? Where are you right now?"

"In my house. I already called the police,

they'll be here soon." Brynleigh chewed on a cuticle. "Colton? I'm scared."

"I'll be right there."

"Ok." Lately, it seemed as if every situation had an emotion attached to it and usually one she wasn't prepared for. "God, this is Brynleigh." Why she had to announce herself didn't escape her. She didn't know if He knew her or not, but if He did and He was so inclined, she could use a little help. If He was orchestrating things like Selena said, maybe He could do a little better with her. She could use a good thing or two her way. But maybe that wasn't how this worked. Maybe she needed to trade something or work harder or be better. Or maybe God couldn't care less about her.

~

Colton's truck rushed around the corner. A cop car sat behind Brynleigh's in her driveway. Thoughts of the night of the fire at her bookstore assaulted him as he entered her house. She huddled near a police officer.

"Brynleigh? Are you okay?" She opened her arms to him, and he readily embraced her. She was shivering, no doubt remembering the fire and her last encounter with the police.

"I'm ok." Brynleigh muffled against his shoulder.

"And you are?" The policeman asked, pen poised over notepad.

"Her personal security." The cop arched his eyebrows at him and nodded. Colton dropped his grip on Brynleigh. Yeah, that sounds stupid. And where were you tonight, Mr. Security? Just trying not to go to jail.

Brynleigh sniffed and turned away.

The officer put gloves on and picked up the brick.

"What's written on the brick?" Colton watched the cop drop it into a plastic evidence bag. Brynleigh shrugged. "Leave."

"Leave what? Your house?"

"I don't know."

"We've taken all of the pictures we need. You don't know what this means or who would want to scare you?" The cop gathered his notepad, evidence bag, and camera.

"No, I really don't."

"We'll look at all of the evidence and get back with you with what we find out."

"Wait. Brynleigh, did you ever hear back about the fire investigation?"

Brynleigh shook her head.

"You had a fire here, too? I don't see any evidence of that." The police officer looked around the room.

"Not here. At my bookstore in Winslot Village."

"That's a different precinct than this one, but we'll touch base with them."

"Okay, thank you."

Brynleigh and Colton watched the officers pull out her driveway. Brynleigh lifted her tear-stained face to his.

"Ummm…can you stay for a minute?" She looked back at the window.

"Brynleigh, I'm not going to leave you to clean

up by yourself." He gave her a half-smile. "Despite what happened tonight, I'm not a monster, I promise."

"I know. I wouldn't have called you if I thought that."

He gently took her hand and pulled her back to the kitchen. He startled when the Tin Man, resting against the wall, caught his eye.

Brynleigh chuckled. "He does that to me, too."

"I was so worried about you I didn't see him the first time I came in."

"I'll get the broom and a trash bag."

Colton nodded. This was a big mess. And a scare tactic. What was going on?

After sweeping and mopping the floor, Colton taped a piece of cardboard to the glass, covering the hole.

"Thank you."

Brynleigh was silent through the motions of cleaning up. He could feel her gears tripping over each other, trying to make sense of the night.

"I think I'm done." Colton put away the broom and put the trash bag with the broken glass out in the garage.

Brynleigh stood in the kitchen.

"Brynleigh?"

"I don't want you to go." She turned and stepped down into the den. "I know that's not appropriate-"

"It's nearly morning. I'll stay and fix the window when it's light out."

Brynleigh plopped onto an overstuffed couch and pulled a blanket around her. "Thank you."

"No problem. Can I start a fire? Would that help?" At her nod, Colton picked up kindling from the wood bin and started a small flame. Looking back at her, he wondered if he should sit in the chair across the room or on the couch next to her. She answered his unasked question by patting the space next to her. He hesitated, knowing she would be so near, so vulnerable, and close enough to–

"Please?"

Colton sat next to her and wrapped his arm around the back of her. She sighed as she burrowed down further in his arm. She was asleep in seconds. Colton gazed at the fire. He never wanted to leave this spot ever.

Chapter Eleven

"Colton?" Brynleigh sat up from the couch. She ran her fingers through her hair in an attempt to calm the mess. She looked around the room, but no Colton. Hearing glass crunching, she moved to the front door, her heart hammering. Was the person who threw the brick in her window back? She tripped over her shoes and fell hitting her head on a table corner. A lump began to form instantly.

"Brynleigh? I ran out to get some– what are you doing on the floor?" Colton nearly tripped over her. Two large Styrofoam cups were in his hands. Putting the coffee on the hall table, Colton bent down to look her in the eye. "Let's get ice on that bump."

Brynleigh sat up against the wall and accepted the ice packet he gave her wrapped in a kitchen towel. She looked up at him and started to laugh.

"What's so funny? Maybe you hit your head harder than I thought." Colton rocked back on his heels.

"Your face looks as bad as mine feels." Brynleigh laughed loudly. "We are a pair."

Colton helped her to her feet and led her to the couch, avoiding the offending shoes. He pulled the kitchen towel back from her face and gently touched the corner of her eye.

"I think you'll survive. The swelling is already going down." He stood and retrieved the coffee mugs. "I saw my face in the mirror and nearly screamed in terror. Two shiners and a split nose. Pretty fantastic."

Brynleigh laughed again.

"Seriously though, I am sorry for what happened last night." Colton hung his head.

"We probably do need to talk." Brynleigh rested her hand on his arm.

"I screwed up. Let him get the best of me." Colton frowned. "Let's talk about you and the brick and what we're going to do."

Brynleigh chewed on a cuticle, letting the ice pack drip onto her shirt. He'd changed the subject. Brynleigh suspected there was a well-protected vat of anger inside of him. "I don't date men with anger issues."

Colton raised his eyebrows and moved away from her. "I don't have anger issues."

"Typically said by someone who does."

"And we're not dating. I'm your security detail which you clearly need based on recent events."

"And as my security, you thought it was necessary to sleep on my couch and bring me coffee?"

"Are you kidding right now? You called me. I just set up an appointment for a company to come fix your glass window. I stayed because you were asleep on my arm," he retorted.

Brynleigh grabbed her phone as it started

ringing. "Colton, please hold. We are not done." She walked into the kitchen, answering the call. "Yes, this is Brynleigh Tavish. Yes, I'm the owner of — Oh, okay. Doesn't explain the brick through my window this morning. Unrelated. Okay. Thanks for calling."

"Was that the police?" Colton stood by the fireplace.

"No."

"Is it something I need to know as your security guy?" He made air quotes with his fingers.

"No. It was before you were my security guy," she mimicked him. "and something I can handle on my own." She avoided his gaze.

Colton picked up his coffee and strode to the door. "See ya Monday."

Brynleigh watched him walk down the sidewalk. If he didn't want to talk about himself, then she didn't want to talk about herself. Two could play that game. What did her mother always say? She was the only one she could depend on.

The fire investigator told her during the phone call they believed a hotpot sitting in the window had been left on and accidentally turned over, starting the fire. Accidentally turned over? More like the people who broke into her store turned it over. They'd downplayed the 911 call indicating she probably just heard the fire noise and thought it was someone breaking in. That was a load of dog-doo. She wasn't a fraidy-cat female jumping at the slightest noise. Someone had legitimately broken into her store while she was in it. She hadn't started to smell smoke until after she was hidden in the storage closet. And the brick through her window? Unrelated? Likely not.

Brynleigh tried to go back to sleep on the couch, but thoughts of Colton kept swirling in her head. A shower might wash away her ugly thoughts about the last twenty-four hours.

It didn't work.

~

Colton slammed his truck door shut. Females were the most confounding individuals. One minute, she needed him. The next minute, she was yelling at him. It didn't help that when she looked at him, two black eyes and a swollen nose looked back at her. Evidence of his inability to control himself. If he couldn't protect himself, how could he ever protect her? He knew that wasn't the truth. He'd always protected his squad…almost always. He'd taken the brunt of the last engagement and it had proved detrimental to him and Bandit.

Colton's phone rang just as he was considering jumping in the shower.

"Hey, Colton. Can you help me up here for a minute?" Mark, his brother, asked.

"Does it involve getting dirty? If so, I'll hold off on the shower."

"Probably, but the horses won't care what you smell like."

Maybe a good ride out in the fresh air would calm his thoughts.

Colton got back in his truck, Bandit in back, and drove up to the barn where his brother was waiting. Billy, the surly kid, was standing next to him, holding the reins of the horse he'd ridden before.

"For all that is good and holy— what happened to your face?" Mark inspected his eyes and nose and handed over the reins of Colton's horse.

Billy watched the exchange, eyes wide.

"This is what crossing me looks like. You should see the other guy." Nothing like a little fear instilled in the kid. He swung up in the saddle and eyed Billy, who followed his example.

"First, I'll say thanks for your help. Secondly, I'll say you look like Dad—"

"Don't," Colton warned. He was nothing like his father. His father used his fists— okay, well, maybe he was a little like him. Wonderful. So grateful for a little brother who reminded him he was just like his father. Of course, he really only had to look in the mirror. "What are we doing exactly?"

"One of the goats got out of the pen, and we can't find it."

"Uh, no. Nope. I'm not a goat wrangler. Told you first thing, I want nothing to do with any goats." Colton got down off the horse.

"You're not going to look for it? That's the kind of man you are?" Billy taunted. He'd recovered quickly after seeing Colton's face. Probably been on the other end of a beating, too.

Colton shook his head. His emotions were bubbling on the red side again, past the gray line of control.

"Please."

Colton shot his brother a look as he swung back in the saddle. "I don't like this. I'm only doing this because… yeah, I don't know why." Colton clicked to his horse, who pranced sideways. He could feel the power and energy behind the big horse's step. They'd run out a ways and see what they could see. Maybe he'd bring the stupid goat back or maybe he'd leave both the goat and the boy and run far and fast to no-man's land.

"How far are we goin'?" Billy asked.

Colton turned around in his saddle. "There's caves up here over the bluff. We'll check there first."

"I don't know what the big deal is about goats."

"It's not with the herd, so apparently, it's lost."

"So? It's just one. Can't be worth much."

Kid had a point. A responsibility was a responsibility, though. "What if I didn't come back with you in tow? You're just one kid."

Billy nudged his horse up next to Colton's, fear in his eyes. "I ain't worth anything. Nobody'd come looking for me."

Colton glanced at him. He was serious. What had happened with this kid to make him think like that? Never mind. Don't feed the animals. He should have had a comforting word for the boy, but he had nothing. "Well, it appears we're more alike than I thought."

Billy gave him a sideways look. "Nobody wants you either?"

"I've been told that before. Look, I'm not up on God like my brother is…" How to finish that sentence. Colton looked over the horizon. From their vantage point on a small hill, they could see the caves stretching out below them. A lone gray coyote circled the opening of one of the caves. "Looks like we've found our goat."

Billy followed his point and stood still, only his horse's ears moved.

Colton pulled his Winchester out of the holster.

"Are you going to shoot it?" Billy whispered.

"Be ready to ride. And hold onto your horse. He may spook." Colton pointed the gun up in the air and fired. Both horses slid sideways, running into each other.

"Come on." Colton slapped the reins down on his horse's neck and galloped to the cave the coyote had vacated. Billy rode close behind.

Colton slowed his horse and stopped at the mouth of the cave. "Exactly like I thought." They could hear the goat's bleating cries. "Hop down there and get him."

"And then what? Why don't you do it?" Billy snapped.

Colton looked at the goat and shook his head. He was going to have to do this. As much as he didn't want to, there was no way the kid could balance a goat and keep control of his horse. "Fine, hand it up."

Billy stepped out of the saddle, scooped up the goat and pushed it into Colton's lap.

Colton resisted the urge to curse at him. The goat stopped bleating and lay warm, curled up on his chest. Colton held him there with his free arm. Wasn't exactly what he had in mind. If it'd been a calf, he would have thrown front legs on one side and back legs on the other, behind him on the saddle. The goat smelled. Just like the goats in Afghanistan. But this one was tiny and very unlike the horse-sized ones. Colton's heart hammered and his palms were slick with sweat. The goat shifted. Bile rose in his throat. He was going to lose his breakfast. He took a deep breath, away from the goat. 1…2…3…inhale…1…2…3…exhale.

"Are we leaving or what?" Billy asked.

Colton's eyes shifted back to the kid. He couldn't make his lips respond and his body had apparently stopped reacting to commands. He sucked in a stench-filled breath.

A shape appeared next to his horse. A person. He couldn't see through the haze.

"Colton?" The shape questioned and then laid a hand on his leg, sliding the goat off his saddle.

Colton grabbed the goat. It was slipping. He was slipping. He fell to the ground and vomited.

"Hey, take a sip of this." A voice above him offered a canteen.

He tipped it back and allowed the fresh water to pour into his mouth. He swished it around and spit out the sour taste.

"Thanks." Colton sat back on his haunches.

"No problem."

"Brandon."

"Yep, it's me. I heard the shot and rode over to see what was what."

Just him. Having a little freak-out moment. Colton eyed the goat now on Brandon's saddle. Colton slapped his leg. He was not in Afghanistan, and the goat was more frightened of them than he was of it.

"He was totally tripping." Billy offered.

Great, the kid was still here. Colton wished he'd have run back home and missed the melt down.

"I'll ride home with you." Brandon turned his

horse back to the ranch.

"Thanks."

Billy rode ahead, his horse already smelling home and a handful of grain.

"Got a problem with goats, huh?"

Colton blew out a heavy breath. "Yeah, comes from my time overseas. The goats were regarded as a prized possession and more important than human life. We started taking out their goats one by one with poisoned bread. Not something I'm proud of."

"I can understand that. You were in almost full-blown panic mode." Brandon confronted.

"Thanks for not saying PTSD mode. The response may be due from the trauma we witnessed over there, but I don't have a disorder."

Brandon nodded.

"Is that what happened Friday night, too?"

Sure a lot of questions. Brandon seemed to be able to handle the honest talk, though. He didn't have the same experiences, but they were compatible in other ways, and Brandon was easy to talk to.

"Nope, that's from a whole different period of trauma. My father used to beat my mother. He's in prison, and she's dead." He held the monotone. Enough emotion for one day.

"From your father?"

"What? No. She died of cancer after he went to prison. Unrelated."

"Oh, sorry."

"I guess I'm more like my father than I'd feared." Colton's shoulders slumped.

"You don't have to be."

"Apparently, I am."

"Colton, I can see all that in your eyes. How you loathe talking about your father."

"Wouldn't you be if you saw your father drunk every night, beating up women?" Billy had dropped back beside them.

Colton glanced over at him. The kid's father must have been abusive, too.

"I suspect you think God is like that," Brandon added.

"Worthless–" Both Colton and Billy said in unison.

Brandon tipped his hat at them. "You think God is worthless?"

"No, me. And him." Billy gritted out, nodding at Colton.

"Couldn't be farther from the truth." Reaching the barn, Brandon released the goat into Mark's arms. "Hey, neighbor. Colton, why don't you and Billy come to church tomorrow? We'll grab lunch afterwards."

"We'll see." No chance. Colton shook Brandon's hand. "Thanks for the help."

Chapter Twelve

"**Still going to** church with us, Brynleigh?" Selena's voice was staticky on the line.

"Yes, I'll be ready." Maybe she'd see why Selena treasured God in her life. Could she force Him to work in her favor? Like a big brother in the sky watching out for her? She could use God in her life, especially since she'd asked for His help. Maybe she needed a new introduction to Him.

Brynleigh dressed and took her coffee outside on the patio to wait until Selena and Brandon arrived. This was one of her favorite parts of the day. Birds were chirping their good morning song and others were waking up. A light breeze set the wind chimes tingling and dried up the dew on the grass. She also loved summertime, nearly dusk, with a group of friends hanging out on her outdoor lounge furniture. How would Colton react to an invitation like that? He didn't strike her as a hang-out-with-friends kind of guy. Maybe she should find out. Or not. He'd stormed out yesterday, mad at her for what exactly? Her assumption that he might want to date her? Or the truth about his anger?

"We're here." Selena texted her.

She secured the back door, grabbed her purse and locked the front door behind her. Not that it mattered. The plywood on the window Colton had put up temporarily could easily be pushed in.

"Wow, that is some window. Or lack thereof."

"I know. I'll tell you about it when you drop me off." Brynleigh opened the back passenger door. "Brandon, can you look the other way?"

"What? Oh, of course."

Brynleigh hiked up her skirt and climbed into his large Dodge truck. Selena chuckled as Brandon discreetly looked out the windshield. Getting out of the truck in the church parking lot could provide a show-and-a-half. Thoughtfully, Brandon parked with her door facing the opposite direction.

Entering the sanctuary, Brynleigh took in the large, red-carpeted area, the choir up front and the rows and rows of padded seats. It looked more like a theater than a church, but on a grander scale. The cross at the front and the pulpit in front of it were the only things identifying it as a church.

Selena led her down a hallway and into a smaller area with padded chairs as well, but fewer and in a more intimate setting.

"This is where the first service meets. The more traditional service meets at 11am in the big sanctuary.

Thank goodness. Brynleigh did not want to be in a sea of people. Just the thought exhausted her.

The pastor, a young guy with glasses and a worn Bible, welcomed them from the front. A few simple worship songs and he began the message.

"Please turn to 1 Corinthians 13 in your

Bibles."

Brynleigh squirmed. She did not have a Bible and wasn't even sure if there was one in the house. Thankfully, the words were also shown on the screen behind him.

"Love is patient and kind." The pastor started reading. "Love does not envy or boast. It is not arrogant or rude. It does not insist on its own way. It is not irritable or resentful. It does not rejoice at wrongdoing, but rejoices with the truth."

Wow, that's a lot of 'doesn'ts'. Was this for real? Could someone actually do that? Maybe the type of love was just for special people, people who knew God? Certainly nothing she'd ever encountered.

She glanced at Selena and Brandon, their fingers intertwined. What they had was real, she could feel it every time they glanced at each other. Was that what love looked like?

Brynleigh chewed on her cuticle. She'd never meet anyone who lived that type of love. Colton was kind, but also angry and although he made her heart speed up any time she was in the room with him, she wasn't around him enough to witness any of those other love actions mentioned. She suspected the pastor's love references went deeper than between a husband and wife, not that she was thinking in those lines with Colton. For Pete's sake. She didn't really know what she was thinking. Her thoughts whorled around the whole concept of love.

"I'm going to use the restroom. I'll be right back." Brynleigh whispered to Selena.

"It's to the right in the hallway. Do you want

me to go with you?"

"I'm fine. You stay here." Nice offer, but she needed the space for a minute.

Brynleigh entered the first door on the right. Glancing at a stall, she hesitated, and wished there was another restroom. Sounded like someone was losing their lunch. The stall door opened, and her mother walked out, smoothing her hair.

"Mother?"

Her mother startled. "Brynleigh? What are you doing here?"

"I came to church with some friends. I didn't know…"

"I attended church?" Her mother cut her off. "I go to the traditional, real one at 11am, in case you wanted to fact-check me."

"Well, that, too." Brynleigh waved her hand at the stall her mother had come out of.

"Well, I do." Celeste did not acknowledge the vomiting. "I asked what you were doing here." Celeste carefully washed her hands, avoiding any drips on her silk suit.

Love is not rude. The thought floated through Brynleigh's mind.

"Please put your face back together and stop gawking at me."

Love is not arrogant.

"Brynleigh. Whatever you're doing, stop it."

Love is not irritable.

Brynleigh blinked. So far, her mother had managed to match three of the 'not-love' characteristics.

"Have a great rest of your day, Brynleigh."

Was that really the way a person spoke to their only child? Celeste had never had a motherly vibe and was often downright awful. Unless she was in front of others. Then there was a good show of affection. Fake affection.

Brynleigh walked out and sat on a bench just outside the smaller sanctuary. She could hear the pastor finishing his sermon, "And the greatest of these is love."

Not the kind of love Brynleigh had ever known. It was either a calculated maneuver or a conditional one. Never just for who she was. The closest thing she'd encountered to that kind of love was what she felt when she helped the children at the bookstore. And that was gone.

After a closing song, Brynleigh waited until she met Brandon and Selena coming through the doors.

"Are you okay?"

"Sure. I didn't want to interrupt the sermon twice, so I sat out here on this bench." Brynleigh hedged. It was true, but she also didn't want to mention running into her mother.

"Do you want to get lunch with us?"

"I really should get home. Thank you, though."

Brynleigh climbed into the back seat and pulled her skirt back down to an appropriate length. If she ever came with them again, she'd have to remember to wear slacks next time.

Brandon pulled into her driveway. "Tell me what happened to the window?"

"Someone threw a brick through it Friday night while I was at the rodeo. I called the police, they came out and took a statement. I also called Colton who fixed it for me. Or partially fixed it."

Brandon and Selena exchanged a look.

"Want to see it from inside? The glass shattered all the way into the kitchen."

"Sure."

Brynleigh led the way into the house.

"Why did you call Colton?" Brandon asked.

"Oh, you probably don't know. He has a personal security detail at my work." Brynleigh tore a cuticle. "Me."

"Okay. I did not know." Brandon started. "The Colton that got in a fight at the rodeo?"

"Yes."

"Which explains why you were so mad at him. He was being reckless."

"Yes."

"And why do you need a security detail?" Selena stepped toward her.

"Long story. I work for Celeste Tavish. She's actually my mother."

"Hold on." Brandon sat down on her couch. "I can only handle so many bombs at one time."

"I know. It's a lot." Brynleigh sat in a chair across from him and told them the story from the 911 call to the brick through her window.

"Okay, one, you thought someone was breaking into your store so you called 911." Brandon held up one finger.

Selena lifted two fingers. "Two, you think they started the fire."

Brynleigh nodded.

"Three, you went to work for your mother, who just happens to be the president of Texas

Acquisitions and Development Corporation."

"Well, working for her is kinda misleading. She turned the company over to me because she's sick. I'm the acting president in her absence."

Brandon sputtered. "The acting president? Of one of the most notable companies in Dallas?"

"Yes. Colton was hired as personal security for my mother, and when I became acting president, he has to provide that for me now. That's his role."

"Good night. This is a lot, Brynleigh." Selena gawked at her.

"I know."

"What's your mom like?"

"Not like a mom. A dictator maybe. She checks all of the 'shouldn't be's' on the pastor's list of love traits. She's pretty controlling and manipulative."

"And she just turned the corporation over to you?"

"Yeah. She knows, or thinks she knows, I'll do what she wants. I don't want to be there. It's a race to see what happens first- her returning because I'm terrible or me leaving because I hate everything corporate. And being bossed around, honestly." Brynleigh didn't mention the promise of a new bookstore. Despite what she'd done, secure her future, she didn't want people to think she was in it for the wrong reasons. People didn't know what it took to navigate around her mother and her demands.

"What does Colton think?"

"The Colton who saved me from the fire? Or the Colton who lost his cool and used his fists at the rodeo? Or the Colton who fixed my window and is overly protective at work?"

"All of those Coltons are one guy." Brandon stated.

"Or the current Colton who left Saturday mad because he didn't want to talk about his feelings?"

Brandon snorted. "Girl, I don't know you very well and Colton less, but those waters run deep. There's a lot more to Colton than I think you realize."

"Well, regardless, it sounds like you need protection here at home, too. Do you have an idea of why this is happening?" Selena stood.

"I really don't. I agree security needs to be stepped up until this gets figured out, but I don't know what to do about it." Brynleigh stood, too.

"I invited Colton to come to church today, too, and he said he'd think about it, but I guess he decided not to."

Brynleigh shrugged. How uncomfortable would that have been to sit through a sermon on love with Colton in the same row? Despite the heat in her face and her racing heart, the only sign he had any feelings toward her was how kind he was.

"By the way, still wanting to keep this suit of armor?" Selena brushed knuckles over the metal breastplate.

"If you want it, it's all yours. And I call it the Tin Man."

"I would love to take it home. Can we put it in the truck since we're here?"

"Sure. He scares me daily," Brynleigh laughed.

Brandon picked up the Tin Man while Selena held open the door and walked him out to the truck. Brynleigh thanked them and waved as they backed out of the driveway.

Bye bye, Tin Man. Now to figure out lunch.

~

Colton waited until everyone had left the ranch for church before showing life at his house. Regardless of the boys' upbringing, that was the one constant, along with daily chores, Mark required. Everyone had to go to church on Sunday. He'd disregarded that rule just like he had ignored Brandon's invite to church. He took the cap off the meds bottle and swallowed four of the capsules. His face was stretched tight across his nose and the pain behind his eyes was almost tolerable.

He let Bandit out for his morning break, fixed a simple breakfast of toast and cereal and settled into his old recliner. He hoped his injuries were a little less aggravating in the morning. He'd see Brynleigh first thing and then maybe disappear for a while. As long as she was in the building and didn't leave without him knowing, she was safe. Seems like the security detail should be the other way around. She was safest at the office, but not at home. She was a complete enigma to him. Beautiful, savvy, quick-witted, warm most of the time. He was opening up to her little by little. He'd shown some pretty ugly sides of himself to her, too. What must she think of him now? He'd know tomorrow. She was guarded and professional at work.

Colton found his baseball glove and walked down to the barn, Bandit joyfully picking up sticks along the way. He set fresh bottles up on the half wall and backed up the length to a pitcher's mound.

Zinging the baseball at the bottles created a satisfying crash as it connected with the first one in the row. Three more down and his throwing arm was beginning to burn. It felt good to stretch out and let the ball fly from his hand.

"Whatcha doing?" Billy stood next to the barn.

Colton looked around at him. "You back from church already?"

"Short service today. Youth pastor was preachin'."

"What does that mean?"

"Means the youth pastor only knows how to preach short sermons 'cuz we have short attention."

"Got it." Colton lobbed the ball to him. "Have you got a mitt?"

"What do I need one for?"

"I want to set up scenarios to see how good you really are."

The boy's chest puffed out. "Better than you."

"Then go get your glove, hotshot."

"Don't call me that," Billy called over his shoulder as he ran for the house. The lanky boy was back quickly and watched Colton mark off perimeters. "What is this?"

"Here's the pitcher's mound and where that flat piece of plywood is, the catcher's box." Colton pointed out the other markers. First base, third, second. At each base, he soft lobbed the ball to Billy. Every time, he caught it squarely in his mitt. "That's really good catching."

Billy shrugged.

"Trade me places. You pitch to me." Colton walked in. "This is a little different than the wall. You've got a window you can pitch to." He motioned between chest and his knees. "More of a zone."

"I know, I know." Billy stood ready on the mound.

Colton squatted and watched for him to throw the ball. A couple of seconds clicked by. "Whatcha waiting on?"

"The play. What kind of ball do you want?"

Colton stood. "Any kind?"

"One finger is for a fastball," the boy raised his index finger, "two for a slider, and three is a curveball."

"Okay." Colton squatted again. Let's see what the kid's got. He gave the signal for a fastball. Yep, that was fast. Colton threw the ball back. In position, he gave a two-finger signal.

"I can't see what you want," Billy yelled, "that's why they wear polish on their nails."

"We're playing catch, dude." Colton stood again. "And you have black fingernail polish on, not white," he yelled back. He changed the signal to a curveball.

"Not me, you." The boy wound up and let the ball fly, beaning Colton on the head.

"Get down, get down." Colton could hear his voice, but everything darkened and went black.

Clawing at the dirt, Colton dropped to his knees and then flat on his belly. Hands over his head, he listened for gunfire. Real still now and they'll think you're dead. It's going to be okay. It's going to be okay. As the fog began to clear his brain, Colton focused on the tennis shoes beside him. Dirty, kids' shoes, not military-issued boots. Colton blinked and tried to sit up.

"Colton, please stay still." His aunt, not his

sergeant, pleaded.

"What in the Sam Hill happened?" His brother's shoes came into view.

What was the kid yelling at him? He didn't mean it?

"You don't believe me, do you? You don't. No one ever does."

Colton sat up despite his aunt's protests. He stared at Billy now standing above him, hands balled at his side.

"Boy," Colton started with effort.

The boy shuddered.

"You have a heck of an arm."

Aunt Eunice snorted and returned to the house.

Billy sank to the ground next to Colton. Mark looked them over and followed their aunt into the house.

"I really didn't mean it," Billy whispered, "no one ever believes me, but I really didn't."

Colton reached out to touch the boy's shoulder, who flinched.

"Go ahead. Hit me. I deserve it."

"Billy, look at me." Colton tilted his head back as far as he could without sending blinding heat down his forehead, past the split nose. "One, I do believe you. Two, no one deserves to be hit, and three, you didn't mean to throw the baddest curveball your catcher signaled you to throw?"

The boy met his eyes. "Why did you yell at me to get down?"

"I said that?"

Billy nodded his head.

Colton reached out his hand, and the boy

helped him stand. "Help me to the house. I need to get some ice on my face. My whole face."

Chapter Thirteen

"Good morning." Brynleigh greeted the security guard, cooly ignoring Colton standing next to him, in the lobby. He could probably see through the tons of makeup she'd applied to the bruise on her forehead, and her face flushed hot. Colton and the guard stopped laughing when she approached. Better be laughing about how Colton's face got rearranged and not about her. Neither were funny in her opinion.

Colton turned and followed her into the elevator. No one said a word until they reached her office.

"This what we're doing now? Not speaking?" Brynleigh took off her coat and hung it behind the door.

"What would you like to talk about?" Colton remained at attention just inside her office.

"Fine." Brynleigh plunked down in her office chair and spread some papers out on her desk. Why was he still looking at her? She wasn't a specimen under a microscope. Brynleigh started to giggle. The image of her under a microscope like the frogs they had dissected in high school biology class was too much. Or maybe she was stressed. Or maybe she was losing it under the confines of the business, the fire, the brick, and now Colton stoically staring at her.

"Well, it's odd, but I'll take laughter over the silent treatment." Colton sat on one of the couches.

Brynleigh laughed out loud. "Sorry, I think the stress is getting to me."

"Can't imagine why. Look, can we start out right side up this week?"

"I'm not sure what that means, but yes, we can only go up from here."

"The window repairman is supposed to come today. Okay if I meet him at your house and oversee getting it installed?" Colton offered.

"That would be really nice. I feel like I need to spend time in the office." Brynleigh glanced up at him. Despite the damage to his face, he was still achingly handsome. Brynleigh shivered, thinking about the two of them falling asleep on her couch. He may have a temper, but it was always directed at the right things. Like the guy at the rodeo who disrespected his girlfriend. Colton didn't have the self-control to ignore injustice. Not a bad thing, but handling it with his fists was not the first response. Or shouldn't be. Brynleigh wondered what he had been like in the military. Was he constantly in fights? Or did he reserve the anger for when it mattered, like saving civilians or protecting the guys under him? Brynleigh lowered her lashes when she realized she had been looking at him for several seconds, lost in thought. He gave her a devilish grin. He'd caught her staring.

He coughed in his hand, forcing her to look up

at him again. This time, she held his gaze.

"I'll need your house keys."

"Oh yes, of course." Brynleigh dug them out of her purse. "Thank you."

"No problem. Please don't leave the building while I'm gone."

"What if you're not done in time and I'm ready to leave?"

"Just call me so I know where you're at."

"Do I need a tracker so you know where I am at all times?"

Colton cocked his head to the side. "Not a bad idea. Or we could download an app that tracks you."

"No, I don't think that's necessary." She did not want someone monitoring her every movement. How controlling would that be?

With a mock salute, Colton left her office, leaving behind the faint trace of his cologne. Brynleigh spent the remainder of the morning looking over spreadsheets, future projects, and boring reports.

Late in the afternoon, Brynleigh decided enough for the day. Her eyes were crossed from looking at financial reports, and she was barely able to keep her head off her desk. The candy bar and diet soda she'd had mid-afternoon had the opposite effect and contributed to her fatigue. At one point, she had seriously considered shutting her office door and lying down on the couch for a brief power nap. What would her mother think? There was only so much corporate a girl could take in one day.

She texted Colton she was on her way home. Thankfully they were almost done and he'd return her keys to him when she arrived. When she pulled into the drive, a beautiful seamless window greeted her, and all of the breakage debris was cleaned up.

"Wow, looks fantastic." Brynleigh went inside where Colton was standing looking out at her.

"It does look good. They'll send you the bill later today so you can turn it into your insurance company. I would have paid for it, but you know, security doesn't pay very well." He grinned at her. His standard uniform of black pants and black shirt had been exchanged for a well-fitted T-shirt under a flannel shirt, jeans, and scuffed work boots. Brynleigh liked both looks. He was pretty perfect in uniform, casual, or all dressed up.

"How about you stay for dinner? That'll be my thanks to you."

"You don't have to do that."

Brynleigh took the broom. "Sure I do." They brushed hands, and her heartbeat sped up.

"Come on, stay for dinner."

"Okay. I can be persuaded. What are you fixing?" Colton leaned back against the counter.

"Chicken Fried Steak, mashed potatoes, and home-grown green beans." Brynleigh checked off on her fingers.

"Wow, that's impressive. For some reason, I didn't think you could cook."

Brynleigh snorted. "I can't. But DoorDash has a wonderful selection of food for our perusal."

Colton laughed. "And there it is, folks. She can't cook."

"Nope, not in my repertoire." She brought out a stack of menus. "I can warm up the green beans, though. They come from a friend's garden." She laid the menus on the counter behind Colton which put her in closer proximity to him than she'd intended.

Colton caught her wrist. "Maybe I can cook dinner tonight."

Brynleigh chewed on her bottom lip, still in his grasp. She stepped closer to him. "In my kitchen?" Her voice cracked like a twelve-year-old girl's. His warm fingers on her wrist sent her heartbeat into overdrive. She was sure he could feel it, too.

"Yes." He reached out and captured her other hand.

Brynleigh locked eyes with him.

"Show me what you've got to work with, and I'll do my magic." He let go of her and moved over to the fridge.

His magic? It was already working, surrounding her with a giddy schoolgirl crush.

~

This lady was going to be the death of him. She was soft and he hadn't wanted to let go of her. She was still his boss. And the magic? Colton shook his head. She was smart, good-looking, feisty, and … his boss. Until that status changed somehow, he had to keep his wits about him and not fall victim to her charm. Sometimes when she looked at him, there was a longing in her gaze and a desire of his to reach out and hold her. He needed to be much more in control with his feelings than he was with his fists.

"You've got some surprise meat in here." Colton pulled the package out of the freezer and showed her the freezer burned meat.

"That about sums up my cooking skills."

"You've got fixings for soup and salad. Does that interest you?"

"Whatever you're fixing, I'll eat."

"Okay, how about potato soup with crunchy bread and a mixed salad?"

"Sounds amazing." Brynleigh jumped up on the counter and gave directions to where her utensils were.

Colton noticed her long legs hanging over the counter as she casually watched him. He enjoyed being close to her as he peeled potatoes into the sink.

"Colton?"

He continued peeling the potatoes, convinced if he looked up at her, he would drop everything, take her face in his hands and kiss her soundly.

"Colton?"

"Yes?" He turned and moved a safe distance away before looking at her.

"Do you know why I agreed to run Texas A&D for my mother?"

Colton blew out a breath. Safe territory.

"Not really. Doesn't sound like who you are."

"My mother is ruthless and controlling and powerful, things I never, ever want to be. My little community bookstore was a disgrace to her at the worst and a dislike at best. But she's sick, really sick, certifiably- I know, I checked with her doctor- sick."

Colton continued fixing dinner.

"After the fire, I was at a loss about what to do next. I loved working in the community and contributing to society in small ways. I loved having the kids come in and watching the light bulb come on when I explained a subject they were struggling with.

I loved all of that. But then the fire…"

"Seems pretty convenient for the village to be closing down and then your fire and then this opportunity arose." Colton suggested.

"You think all three were connected?"

"I don't believe in coincidences." Colton watched her spin a curl around her finger.

"I'm not sure. Anyway, with the corporation, I feel like I may be able to bring my own touch to it, my flavor. Plus, it's not a permanent thing. She'll be back, I hope." The new bookstore seemed trivial at this point. Colton would not understand.

Colton grinned at her as he added salt and pepper and milk to the sizzling bacon in the pot.

"I'm not into casinos and hotels and big land acquisitions, but I know they bring jobs to the area."

"And are the things your mother's corporation is known for."

"Yes. There are smaller things the corp can be involved with that gives back to the community. Or at least pour their money into."

"I'm thinking one of your vice presidents would not be in favor."

"Yeah, Lucas is all about the money and prestige, isn't he?" Brynleigh jumped off the counter and pulled plates and silverware out to set the table. "I have thoughts about him, but I don't really know him yet."

"Go with your gut." Colton put the lid on the soup. "It'll be about twenty minutes or so until the potatoes are soft."

"What should we do while we wait?"

Colton looked at her. Ideas of what they should

do while they waited were screaming through his head.

"Cards? Board game?"

Not what he had in mind. Self-control. Be cool.

"Yes. Great idea."

If he were reading her right, she was relieved. Thank goodness she couldn't read his mind... or could she?

"Gin Rummy?"

"Sure."

Colton beat her numerous times, to her chagrin, before the timer dinged. They loaded up their plates and bowls with potato soup, salad, and bread hot from the oven.

"Colton?"

He looked up from his plate, spoon midway to his mouth. He loved how she said his name. Her eyes were luminous in the soft light above the dining room table. Colton's heart rate quickened. He could sit and stare at her for hours.

"Yes?"

"Thank you for this. For the window, for dinner, for everything." She reached over the table and put her hand on his. "I mean it."

Colton sucked in a breath through his nose. His insides did a little jig. Be cool. Before the thought could fully develop in his brain, he took her hand and wove his fingers through hers. "It's my pleasure." Show restraint. Remember, she's your boss. He released her fingers and put his hands in his lap, emotions running very close to his heart. Brynleigh chewed on a cuticle.

"You're bleeding." Colton jumped up, nearly spilling his soup.

"What? Oh." Brynleigh stuck the offending finger in her mouth.

"Let me see." Colton coaxed her finger out into the light. She had, indeed, chewed a chunk of her cuticle off and blood was running down her finger. He carefully wound a napkin around the bloody fingertip like she'd had when they'd met after the gala. "Brynleigh, I-" He was standing way too close to her and his desires must have shown on his face.

"Colton, stop."

Colton's forehead creased. Stop? Stop what? Stop talking and kiss her? Stop taking care of her? Stop what?

Brynleigh brushed her lips across his cheek and pulled away from him.

Colton stood very still, everything in him, humming. He wanted to pull her back to him. He wanted to kiss her. He wanted all those things, but knew in his heart, they were still in the precarious position of boss to employee and nothing had changed. Except for his feelings for her. Those had moved radically in the space of a couple of hours spent in her company.

"I should go. My boss is a real taskmaster." He winked at her.

Laughing, she moved to the door. "Thank you again. For everything."

He brushed past her into the night air, hiding his impulse to take her in his arms.

"Goodnight, Colton."

"Yes, goodnight." He strode to his truck, aware

she still stood in the doorway. "Get some sleep. I'll see you in the morning."

Driving away, Colton shook himself. Would there ever be a time when he could openly adore her and lavish her with everything she desired? He was falling hard for Brynleigh, and his emotions were as charged up as his heart was tied to her.

Chapter Fourteen

The next morning Colton wasn't at his normal station waiting for her to arrive. Brynleigh had slept less than great, tossing and turning, her touch-and-go dreams conjuring up the blue-eyed man who'd fixed her dinner last night. She was surprisingly relieved to have time to get her emotions in check. His close proximity set off bells and whistles and clanging gongs and loud drumbeats that could only be her heart. Kind, sweet, protective, and her hero on numerous occasions, Colton was beginning to be part of the fabric of her life she'd never expected. Sure, he had his flaws with the fighting and his careful walls that were slowly coming down. Had she seen desire a time or two? Yes. Did she tread lightly? Yes. And the kiss on the cheek? Purely impulsive. Not treading lightly. More like blowing the spark into a flame. Something raw and bold had poured over her. She had to take a step away from him to regain her balance. She was his boss, for Pete's sake. At least at this moment. Maybe in the future, it wouldn't be the case. But for now…

Brynleigh hung up her jacket and settled into the day's work. Colton came in just as she was opening her computer. She smoothed her sweaty hands on her skirt.

"Good morning." Colton greeted her, and she instantly turned pink. She loved the timbre of his voice.

"Good morning. I was surprised to not see you down by the security point first thing this morning." She looked at him, trying for a nonchalant face.

"I was the first thing you wanted to see this morning?" He teased.

Yes, yes indeed. Wait, no. What was he implying?

"You just weren't in your usual spot."

"Who are the flowers from?" Colton walked over to a beautiful vase filled with fresh flowers.

"Why do you want to know?" Brynleigh sniffed. The bouquet was the perfect mix of wildflowers and roses and hydrangeas. A beautiful arrangement.

Colton balled up his fists and gritted the question out again.

Brynleigh, alarmed by his tone, questioned him back, "Why. do. you. want. to. know?"

"Because you've had several threatening circumstances, and I need to be aware of everything. Maybe you have a stalker, or maybe they're poisonous."

Brynleigh laughed. What ridiculous thoughts. But what if they weren't ridiculous thoughts? He should be kept abreast of everything she did. He was only doing his job. "I bought them for me."

"Why would you do that? And when?"

"I'm going to answer those questions simply

because you're security." She couldn't buy flowers for herself? No one else was going to. Fresh flowers were one of her favorites and she wasn't going to wait for someone to think she was worth a bouquet of flowers. "Because I wanted to. And this morning before work. I stopped by a floral shop."

"I'm sorry, that's just odd. Buying flowers for yourself."

"No, it's not. Do you see anyone else knocking down my door to give me flowers?"

He arched one eyebrow and studied her. Turning on his heel, he left her office. Brynleigh shook. He could've said something along the lines of "everyone should bring you flowers" or "I should have brought you flowers" or "You deserve flowers." No, he just left without another word. Men. She'd never figure them out.

Around lunchtime, Lucas stopped by her office. "Want to grab lunch?"

Brynleigh looked up from her paperwork. Lucas wouldn't have been her first choice for a lunch date, but she was hungry.

"Sounds good. Thanks for the invite." Brynleigh closed her laptop and grabbed her purse.

Lucas walked down to his car, a few steps ahead of her. Brynleigh trailed behind like a sub-servant and not his boss. She bristled at his inconsideration.

Their simple lunch turned out to be not-so-simple as Lucas' tastes ran with the big money buckets. Crab rolls and warm shrimp soup for starters. Brynleigh chose a lighter fare, a seafood salad with buttery crackers and fresh avocado. She attempted small talk, but Lucas was consumed with his food. He treated the waiter badly, making snide comments about the man's hair style and subtle lisp. He ate part of his entree and then sent it back to the kitchen, stating it was now cold. After their meal, Lucas flashed the cash in his wallet and left a meager tip. Brynleigh slid a ten-dollar bill under her plate when Lucas wasn't looking, hoping it would cover her embarrassment and Lucas' bad behavior. She couldn't wait to get back to the office.

"I'm going to go by those properties again." Lucas steered the car expertly with its luxury seats and high horsepower.

"Okay." So much for getting back to the office.

As Lucas approached from the south, the sleek car passed the first ranch where Selena and Brandon lived. Brynleigh knew their ranch wouldn't be affected by the casino, but their western town competitions might be if the corporation expanded its vision. The next ranch over was the one who would suffer the most from the land acquisition. It would need to be completely bulldozed and leveled. What about the man she met and the boys who lived there under court order? Where would they go? The ranch might not be the most favorite community asset, but they were far enough out of town where they wouldn't bother anyone's conscience and the boys could learn responsibilities and be safe from whatever circumstance had gotten them where they were at. It was a win-win situation, in her book. Mark, the owner of the ranch, had been gracious to show her around when she'd visited, and his love for the property and the boys was evident. He'd be shattered if this casino deal went through. She knew how progress happened and the weighty decisions needed for forward movement. Unfortunately, her mother and Vice President Lucas only equated progress with dollar signs.

"What if we turned the property around and the long length went off to the west instead of south?" Brynleigh proposed.

Lucas snorted. "The paperwork and drawings have already been drawn up. We can't change something of this magnitude now."

"So? Change it." She wouldn't be intimidated by him.

"You haven't been with the corporation very long. At least not long enough to understand it."

"Considering Mother turned it over to me," she wanted to add, and not you, "I believe I do know this corporation and I understand the cost of changing things at this point. That ranch is doing good things."

Lucas spun the car around and headed back to the office. "I have no intentions of working together with anyone. Nor do I care what good those people are doing. The drawings stand as written."

"We'll see."

Parking next to her car, Brynleigh got out, thanked him for lunch, and joined him in the elevator. First thing, check on that property and see if it was, indeed, too late to change.

"Juliette, can you check on something for me? This really isn't in your wheelhouse, but I'm hoping you can help me. Or at least point me in the right direction." Brynleigh stepped into Juliette's office. She lowered her voice on the off chance the walls between the vice presidents' offices weren't heavily insulated. "Lucas said this piece of property is being bought for the new casino." She pointed to a plot on her phone. "Can you see where the land acquisition process is right now?"

"Certainly. I should be able to pull it up on the server." Juliette lowered her voice, too. "Why are we whispering?"

"I just have a feeling about it and I'm not sure Lucas would like my viewpoint on it."

Juliette raised her eyebrows and pursed her lips.

"Okay, it says here that…" Juliette paused.

"What? What does it say?"

"Come here and look at this." Juliette turned her computer screen as far as it could towards Brynleigh.

"What am I looking at?" Brynleigh scrolled down the contracts and maps to the bottom.

Mark Bruens, Owner.

"Isn't that-"

"Colton's last name?" Brynleigh's pulse began beating behind her eyes. Colton's brother owned the ranch Texas A&D was trying to bulldoze? That was a complication she hadn't anticipated.

~

Colton stomped down the hallway looking like a rooster that went through a car wash. His hair stood on end from nervously running his fingers through it a hundred times. Of all the nerve… she couldn't stay put in the office? She felt safe leaving with Lucas? And not telling him? How was he supposed to do his job if she wouldn't communicate with him? She didn't have to ask permission. Letting him know would be sufficient. Not really, though. He would have told her no or would have gone with them. It was like a slap in the face. She'd rather go with Lucas alone even with her trepidations than tell him she was leaving the building. Was she trying to spin him out, make him worry? Keep him from doing what he was hired to do?

He spotted Lucas' car pulling into the parking garage. Give it a minute and then go confront her. She needed to know how confusing she made his job. She'd been mad at him for the flowers thing, but enough to jump in the car with Lucas without telling him? Taking the stairs to give himself time to calm down, he checked her office first. Not there. He headed to Lucas' office, sweat beading down his back.

He stopped at Juliette's office when his eye caught Brynleigh was leaning over a computer screen. She was safe. Nothing happened out of the ordinary. She went for a ride with the vice president, who Colton didn't fully trust or like- a vibe the guy gave off, one that made Colton wary. They both startled when he charged in. Quickly closing her computer, Juliette raised wide eyes to him. Brynleigh refused to look at him. What was going on? Colton's neck hairs stood up. The tension in the room was thick and he absentmindedly wiped his hands on his pants. When things were about to get squirrely out in the field he could always trust his body cues to alert him to trouble ahead. He had that same feeling now. He'd busted into the office with every intent to ream Brynleigh for leaving without notifying him, but instead found her on the verge of tears. When she finally did look at him, her lips quivered and moisture threatened to run down her face. Brynleigh's emotional state unnerved him. Gather intel, buddy. Then, make rational decisions. His gut was uneasy, fluctuating with the energy in the room. Juliette didn't look any better with her usually tan face, now pasty white. Brynleigh's eyes darted around him, her glance bouncing off him at random.

"What's going on?" Cautiously, he looked around the room as if it were booby trapped.

"Nothing. We were just going over some things," Brynleigh finally said, scooting around him and fast pacing it to the door. "I'll be in my office if you need anything more, Juliette.

The Vice President nodded.

Colton followed Brynleigh to her office, but was brought up short when she pulled the door shut behind her. Really? She was shutting out her security? What was he supposed to do? Break down the door?

Colton turned on his heel. He'd better take a break and calm down before he unloaded on Ms. Acting President. He'd think clearer after a walk around the building. He backtracked to the elevator and gave Juliette a hard stare as he passed her office.

~

Brynleigh looked in her rearview mirror. Colton was still behind her like he'd been since she left the garage. Apparently, he was going to babysit her at home, too.

If he only knew. Of course, if he knew, he wouldn't be at her house any longer, or at work, or in her life. He couldn't know just yet. The ranch he lived on was directly in the path of the casino, and she may not be able to do anything about it. The blueprints had been in the planning stage before she came on. She was unaware Colton lived on the ranch until she and Juliette had researched the property further. His mother had had the good sense to write out a will naming both sons on the deed. Only when she'd visited it, talked to Mark, and learned about the boys, had she taken an interest in this one project, among twenty others that were also in the planning stages. She might never have known about Colton and the ranch if she hadn't. They were doing good work with the troubled teens and despite dollar signs, this one project didn't feel justified in destroying. Some of the other projects made good business sense and she understood how her mother's corporation profited from them, but this one…this one involved people who were influencing lives. The others were just properties, sometimes only land.

And then to find out it was Colton's home? She wanted to show him she wasn't just out for a buck. He had to know already. But her last name was Tavish, sometimes a curse if people connected it to her mother's cutthroat name.

Apparently, her bodyguard was going to park on the curb instead of behind her car in the driveway.

Brynleigh knocked on his window. "Are you coming in?" She was torn about not wanting him in her home, but also wanting time with him. Her knowledge of the ranch and his closeness would be her undoing. He'd been mad when she'd left with Lucas, but she'd been perturbed at him earlier by the whole flower bouquet conversation. Which was totally opposite from the night before when they had left each other, feelings unspoken and yet tangible and raw and maddening. Brynleigh wanted to pull her hair out. They couldn't get on the same page and the roller coaster ride refused to slow down. Moving to the top of the ride, she expected him to kiss her and then plunged into a valley when some other emotion forced its way in. He was either angry with her, smitten with her, or protective of her. Sometimes all three at the same time.

And how did she feel about him? Well, she was on the same ride as he, on that roller coaster. One minute, she was infuriated with him, the next, wanted him to show her that love was different than what she'd witnessed with her mother. Everything was conditional with Celeste. Which is why she might be able to turn things around on the casino deal. She had to appeal to that side of Celeste. Manipulation was the name of the game with her. Maybe, just maybe, she could turn the tide and Colton would never know it was Texas A&D that wanted to force them to sell. Or better yet, what if she could…

Brynleigh startled when Colton rolled down his window. She'd had a whole conversation in her head while standing by his vehicle. He must think she was off her rocker.

"Brynleigh…"

His tender voice caused her to tear up. She'd find a way out of this mess, somehow.

~

"Brynleigh," Colton had to roll down his window to get her attention. She had been deep in thought and despite how much he wanted to ream her out for leaving with Lucas, she looked like tears could drop out of her eyes at any moment. "I'm not coming in. I'll stay out here tonight so you'll be safe, but I'm not coming in."

"Why not?"

Why not, indeed. Because he'd be so distracted by her, he might miss saving her from more harm. And there's the real reason, folks. He wouldn't, couldn't tell her that, though. No way. He had never, in his life, been so conflicted. Emotions were not his thing. A man did not leave his heart open to be stomped on. Is that what he thought she would do? No, not intentionally. But things still happened, even if they weren't intentional. Better to play it safe and stay in the car.

Brynleigh stomped off only to return in an hour with warm chocolate chip cookies. Colton almost laughed at her. She was trying really hard to get back on his good side. Little did she know, it would take a lot to keep him angry at her for very long. He rolled down his window again, accepted the whole plate, and rolled it back up again.

"Rude. Just rude," she yelled loud enough for him to hear her in the car. She turned back and looked at him before walking into the house, a slight smile on her face.

Yeah, she was distracting. With her hair down, and an oversized T-shirt on over sweats, she was still distracting. Colton shook his head. It was going to be a long night with that image in his head and Brynleigh so close.

Chapter Fifteen

Colton's truck was no longer at the curb when Brynleigh opened the shades of her front window. She'd planned to take him coffee to see if he was in a better mood, but he'd already left. She needed the coffee, having not slept well, despite knowing he was out there keeping her safe. Knowing he was outside her door had the opposite effect she was hoping for. She wondered all night if he was thinking about her as much as she was him. If he'd have come inside, though, she might have told him everything. She needed time, time to see if she could turn this thing around.

At the office, she noticed Colton was in his usual spot, and he followed her into the elevator.

"Thanks for the cookies."

"It was nothing. They were store bought." She couldn't even be nice to him? Once again, she'd put her foot in her mouth. The wall around her heart was in a constant state of flux with him. Two bricks up, one row down. Three rows up, a heart-sized hole down.

She thought she heard him chuckle, but refused to look at him. His blue eyes would see right through her wall as if it were transparency film and not solid bricks.

"I need to stop in and see Juliette for a minute." Brynleigh ducked into Juliette's office and shut the door. "I don't understand it, and I don't like what I don't understand."

"Charlotte's Web. Did Colton stay at your house last night?" Juliette sat on the couch next to her.

"Outside, until sometime this morning. I didn't see him leave." Brynleigh ripped off another cuticle. She shook her head. "I don't know what I'm going to do."

"You haven't told him?"

"No, of course not. Do you think he'd be here if I had?"

Juliette clucked in agreement.

"What's the possibility of figuring out another solution? One that doesn't involve bulldozing the ranch?"

"The casino is going to be pretty lucrative. Lucas has been working on that project for a long time. It stands to gain him a lot of cash."

"I tried during our lunch yesterday to get him to see a different possibility, before I knew who owned the ranch. Do you think I should try again?"

"All you can do is have a conversation with him."

"Before Colton finds out. I'm surprised he didn't push the issue yesterday when he came into your office."

"Brynleigh? Be careful. Lucas is pretty powerful, your mother is cutthroat, and Colton is itching to kill someone."

When Brynleigh opened the office door, she couldn't see Colton so she stepped next door to Lucas' office.

"Yes?"

Lucas barely acknowledged her as if she wasn't the Acting President. His brisk tone rubbed her wrong like sandpaper, and she wanted very much to box his ears to get his attention. Her mother would have rectified that tone in a hurry.

"Sorry to interrupt…" Sorry, not sorry. "I need a minute to continue our discussion from yesterday." She spoke with authority, but it fell flat. It was so important he listened to her argument on this project. Unfortunately, she couldn't approach him with humanitarian persuasion, or community-oriented ones. Her pleas would be dismissed as frivolous and simple. He was all about the money and prestige. She had to present from that angle, as much as she disliked doing so. "The casino project we drove by. I've been thinking about it and I really believe we can kill a couple of birds with one stone."

Lucas barely looked up at her.

"If I could prove turning the project slightly to the east, bypassing the ranch on the corner, would bring in more profit, what would you say?"

Lucas jumped out of his chair and slammed his hand down on the desk. Shocked by his sudden movement, Brynleigh backed up to the door.

"No." The word exploded from his lips.

"I just think…"

"I said No."

"You know, I think you are forgetting who

you're speaking with." Brynleigh stepped forward into his personal space. Her temper flashed and she raised her voice. "I am the acting President of this corporation and even if you think you know what's best, you will at the very least listen to what I have to say."

"I am very aware you are only acting as the president, and your mother is still very much in charge." Lucas raised his voice to match her level and stepped closer to her. She could smell the coffee on his breath. "I am not concerned about who or what is on that property. I don't care whether or not it is helping snotty-nosed kids not go to jail. I do not care if you want to save this poor ranch. I don't." His voice was thundering now. The whole office floor should be able to hear him.

"You should care…"

"I DON'T."

Lucas' office door popped open, and Colton strode in. "Enough. What's going on? Everyone can hear you yelling for half a block."

Brynleigh and Lucas stepped away from each other.

"I'll ask again. What. Is. Going. On?" Colton's eyes narrowed at the VP. "Brynleigh? Want to explain?"

"We have some different ideas for a project." Brynleigh moved towards the door.

Lucas snorted. "You won't get your way on this. That ranch has to go."

Brynleigh blanched, scooted around Colton, and ran for the sanctuary of her office. She passed Juliette in her doorway and gave her a tearful glance.

She attempted to shut the door, however, Colton stuck his foot in the crack and heaved it open.

"Not again. We're not doing that again."

Brynleigh sank down on the couch.

"What were you two yelling about? Why are you so upset?"

Disrespected, that's why she was upset. And devastated. Devastated, she wouldn't be able to keep this news from Colton. Brynleigh pulled a tissue out of the box and wiped her eyes. She swallowed hard, bringing relief to the nausea building in her throat.

"Are you going to tell me or not?" Colton paced the room.

Brynleigh started, "I…uh…" She covered her face with her hands and started to sob. "I tried, I really did."

"Tried what?" Colton sat down next to her. He pulled her hands into his. "All I heard was yelling, and now you're crying. Tell me what happened so I can help. I've always been there for you, you know. There's very little we can't handle together, you know that. But I have to have all of the intel. And you're fighting me the whole way."

Brynleigh shook her head and took her hands from his. "Not after this. You'll hate me now."

"Pretty strong word. And I doubt it. As much as we argue, I know I'm starting to kinda like having you around. It's scary sometimes, how much I do like you, but it's truth."

Brynleigh began crying in earnest, unable to speak. He had shared his feelings toward her, and she was going to crush him. Her feelings had grown, too, but this would be the death of anything, romantic or friendship, between them.

"We were arguing about a piece of property," her voice came out high-pitched.

"Okay. You knew you would probably run into conflict with Lucas at some point. Plus, we both know he's a little shady and a lot like your mother. What property?"

"Yours."

~

Colton fell back on the couch. He ground his teeth, unable to utter any words.

"I'm so sorry. I made several different proposals..."

Colton's blood pressure rose, and his mouth went dry. The boil within neared the explosion level.

"Please say something." Brynleigh pleaded.

Colton jumped off the couch. "What would you like me to say? Huh? I'm grateful for your attempts? You tried? Are we talking about the ranch I live on?"

"I am."

Colton choked on her muffled response. "I suppose to make way for a high rise or a casino or some other obnoxious building Texas A&D can make money from."

"A casino."

"After all we talked about at your house, you didn't have the nerve to tell me then? You just kept talking about me being your hero and how many times I saved you, but didn't mention you were stealing the ranch from me?"

"I'm trying to save your ranch."

"Not hard enough. All of this... I don't know... closeness... friendship, whatever you want to call it, was you buttering me up so we'd sell the ranch? Is that how your momma raised you? Answer me."

Brynleigh shrank back into the cushions.

"Well, that is answer enough." Colton slammed the door on his way out. That door could stay closed now. Forever. He'd opened the office door in hopes of consoling her and had ended up nearly breaking it to get out of there. Funny how the door lined up with his heart. He'd almost declared deep feelings for her, and this was how she repaid him? She truly was her mother's child. Colton's stomach churned and he kicked over the hallway trash can. Done. Done with Texas A&D. Done caring what happened to her. Done with her, period.

~

Brynleigh watched his truck pull into the spot at the curb as the light faded. She hesitated going out there. What was the purpose? To salvage their strained friendship? Or to convince him to listen to her? She didn't know if anything would be right again, but she had to try.

"Colton?"

"What?"

Not very encouraging, but he was here still watching out for her.

"I'm sorry. I'm not done trying, though. Juliette and I had some ideas."

"Juliette knows, too? Am I the last to know?"

Brynleigh shrugged. The night air was as frosty as his attitude. "That was a low blow about my mother."

"If the shoe fits."

"You don't mean that. Do you?"

"I really don't know, Brynleigh. And I'm not interested in finding out."

She could feel the 'anymore' on the end of his statement. "Why are you out here then?"

"Finishing my shift." He handed her an envelope.

"What is it?"

"My resignation. After tonight, you are no longer my responsibility."

"That's all I am to you? A responsibility?"

Colton nodded.

Brynleigh hung her head, scuffing her toe in the dirt at the curb. How did it come to this? She thought she was doing the right thing by trying to keep his land safe, like he had always kept her safe, but she'd only succeeded in causing heartbreak. "Colton?"

Colton sighed. "What, Brynleigh?

"I'm sorry." She turned and shuffled to the house. Maybe she was more like her mother than she'd ever dreamed possible.

Chapter Sixteen

As Colton drove up the lane to the main house, he looked over at the homestead where he and Bandit lived. He took note of the peeling paint and the wobbly railing that could stand a few extra screws. It wasn't perfect, and it was dated, but it held only his memories, and he couldn't imagine living anywhere else.

The main house was chock full of bad and very bad memories. How many times had he walked past the sight of his mother in the back bedroom, laying in the borrowed hospital bed with a scarf as gray as her face, covering the tufts of hair stubbornly clinging to her bald head. Maybe this place should be torn down. Erased.

Two problems came with that resolution. One, his aunt and brother had created a safe haven for the juvenile boys instead of jail. And two, it wasn't just the house the corporation would bulldoze down. It was the whole property- house, land, barn, everything. For the sake of a dollar.

The only safe place on the grounds for him was out behind the barn where that kid had been busting bottles with a baseball. Colton loved playing baseball or a simple game of catch. The pop of the ball in his glove, the stretching out and running your heart out to the bases. Although the memories followed him there, too. One time, he was out by the barn throwing baseballs at the targets and unbeknownst to him, his father had come outside with a pistol. Colton was in the process of a wind up when his father fired the gun, smashing every single target. Colton had hit the ground, thinking his father was aiming at him, embarrassed when he realized what he was really doing. His father had chuckled and walked off. Later, Colton found him in the front room in his easy chair, sleeping in drunken stupor. Colton vowed to always, always be aware of where his father was so that never, ever happened again.

He parked his truck in front of the main house. Maybe Aunt Eunice had made pancakes this morning. That would be the most pleasant thing to have happened in the last twenty-four hours.

"What are you doing out here?" Mark interrupted his thoughts, Bandit busting out beside him.

Colton sat down in one of the porch rockers. He looked down at his hands and frowned. Bandit whined next to him and Colton ran his fingers over his thick fur and his soft ears. "Just thinking."

"Mighty deep thoughts if you're ignoring the smell of bacon. Aunt Eunice says there's still plenty if you want some."

Colton looked up at him. "Do you ever wonder what you'd be doing if this wasn't available to you? Like if they'd made us leave after Dad went to prison and Mom died?"

"Hmm…those are some weighty questions." Mark sat next to him in the other rocker. "Well, we were old enough to take over the property and Aunt Eunice came to stay around that time. Then you enlisted in the military, and you were gone."

"I didn't do it because I wanted to," Colton hung his head.

"Sure about that?"

"I kinda wasn't given a choice after beating up that guy."

"He was an abusive dad that threatened one of your teammates and you couldn't let that happen. Not after our dad."

"Almost landed me in a cell next to him, though."

"But it didn't." Mark rocked back and forth, the morning sun heating up the porch. "What's with all the reminiscing?"

Colton looked at him. "You know, they're wanting to put a casino right next door."

"I know. Is that what this is about?"

"Am I the last person to know?" Colton snorted. "Do you know this? The corporation I'm employed by is the same corporation that wants to buy the land? And how about this… the personal security detail I'm on? Brynleigh Tavish? She's the one running Texas A&D right now. Isn't that a hoot?"

"Is she the pretty strawberry blonde that came out here awhile back? Athletic, sweet?"

Colton blew out a breath. "Why don't I know these things? She was here?"

"She was. Just wanted to see what we do here. I showed her the place, introduced her to the nicer goats, invited her to stay for supper. She declined, but kindly." Mark whistled. "She's your security detail? As in her bodyguard? Why does she need a bodyguard?"

"Not anymore, I'm not."

"She seemed awfully nice. And pretty."

Colton shrugged.

"I see. There was something more between you two than just work."

"Not anymore." Colton sighed. "Once I found out she wanted to bulldoze our property, I told her she was on her own."

"Why did she need a bodyguard?" Mark repeated.

"It was originally for her mother, Celeste Tavish, because I guess she's pretty cutthroat and always stirring up someone's bees. Celeste got sick and turned everything over to Brynleigh temporarily."

"And Brynleigh's cutthroat like her mom?"

Colton's chest tightened. He'd said that to her himself. Or words similar. He hadn't meant it, but he was so angry with her. By her reaction, his words cut deep. Colton put his face in his hands. "No, she's not like that."

"So, she was just carrying out her mother's wishes?"

That sounded a little too easy.

"She said she was going to try and turn it around, but I found out and didn't give her a chance to say how she thought she could do that." Colton ran his fingers through his hair. "There's a vice president up there I don't trust who could be putting pressure on her, too. I don't know. And she's had a string of bad luck lately. Her bookstore burned down, someone threw a brick through her window… this whole thing is too much drama for me."

"Sounds like she does need a bodyguard. Maybe you should hear her out." Mark turned from talking to Colton and yelled at Billy, carrying a baby goat. "What are you doing?"

"He won't eat." Billy dropped the goat in Colton's lap.

"Billy," Colton yelled, startling all of them. "Get him off me. Right now."

The baby goat flopped down on Colton's stomach and pushed his nose under the flap of his flannel shirt.

"He looks pretty content. Can you try to feed him?"

Billy held out the bottle filled with goat's milk. Colton squinted sideways at Mark.

Colton took the bottle and squeezed some out on the tip and then offered it to the baby. Mark and Billy exchanged surprised glances when the goat took the bottle right away.

"Look, you're a goat whisperer," Billy mumbled.

"That's it. I'm not a goat whisperer. I'm not the brunt of your stupid joke. I'm not this goat's nurse." Colton jumped up, dropped the baby goat into Mark's lap and whistled for Bandit. He shouldn't have let Billy leave the goat with him. The baby was definitely tiny and nothing like the large, ugly ones over in Afghanistan. This one needed his help. It was natural for him to try to get the baby to take the bottle. The kid's comment was out of line. He jumped in his truck and slammed the door. His insides growled as he stomped into his house and fell on the bed. No pancakes today. Just blessed sleep. And a handful of painkillers. This day couldn't be over quick enough.

~

When Brynleigh woke, Colton's truck was gone. Fine by her, he hadn't wanted to talk to her anyway. Just turn in his resignation and be done. That's all he wanted. Or all he said he wanted. He'd avoided her eyes during their conversation. Maybe it was more than the ranch situation. Maybe he was also shutting down any possibility of a real friendship. Or more.

There could have been something between them, if and when, she was no longer his boss. There were times when he looked at her with almost a longing. Or they'd hold each other's gaze for a little longer than necessary. Her body and emotions told their own story any time he was near, too.

Another reason to be angry with her mother. She crushed dreams. And any hope of having a normal, fulfilling life free from unrealistic expectations and manipulation.

How amazing would it be to have Colton fix dinner in her kitchen on a regular basis or play cards with. Despite the odds against them, she could see how he might fit in nicely with her future. Unless she was stuck at Texas A&D forever. Or if they bulldozed his ranch to the ground. He'd never forgive her even if she tried until the last second to turn it around and put the casino somewhere else.

"Hello?" Brynleigh answered her cell phone on the first ring. No one called her this early in the morning.

"Good morning, Brynleigh. Just wanted to give you a heads up. An emergency meeting has been scheduled for 10 am this morning. Wanted you to be aware." Juliette sounded apologetic.

"Okay. Who called the meeting?"

"Lucas."

"Well, this should be interesting. I'll see you at my regular time." Great, now what was he up to? Their argument yesterday had been pretty heated.

Brynleigh hurried with her dressing, choosing a colorful skirt with a long jacket. The heels were high, but looked great with the skirt, and she could always exchange them later after the meeting. Sliding a pair of flats in her bag, Brynleigh locked the door and walked out to her car.

As she unlocked her car door, she noticed a brownish fluid coming from under the vehicle. What is that? She bent down and touched the liquid with a fingertip. It smelled like fish oil. She wrinkled her nose. It was the wrong color for coolant, and she knew from an air conditioner leakage on a previous car that coolant smelled sweet. This was a slick, fish smell. Hesitant, Brynleigh opened the car door and sat down. The fire and brick flashed through her thoughts. Surely, this wasn't cause for concern. Colton had been out front all night, hadn't he? There wasn't time for someone to tamper with her car. She would have seen someone lurking about, wouldn't she? Calm down. It was probably nothing.

Hopefully, it was nothing. Maybe she would double check with Colton to see how long he was outside her house. As she picked up her cell phone, her eyes landed on his resignation letter. No, she couldn't call him. He was done with her. Maybe he'd decided sometime in the night to just leave. Leave her exposed to more danger? That didn't seem like him, either, regardless of how mad she made him. He'd made it clear, though, after last night, she was no longer his responsibility. Maybe he'd cut and run early.

"Selena? Sorry for calling so early, but can I talk with Brandon for a minute?"

A sleepy sounding Brandon answered. "Brynleigh? Are you okay?"

"I'm not sure. I woke up this morning and there's this brownish fluid leaking out from under my car."

"Isn't Colton there?"

"Uh, no. He was, but then he left. I don't know when. He came after dark, sat out in his car, and then left before I got up." No reason to mention their huge fight.

"Can you call him back? I doubt he's far from you. Maybe he's grabbing breakfast or already at the office."

"Yes, no. He resigned. He no longer works for me."

Silence on the other end.

"I'll be right there. Don't go anywhere in that car."

"Thank you." Brynleigh disconnected the call. If she only could call Colton. He'd probably still come, begrudgingly, but it was in his nature to be the protector. Brynleigh looked at her watch. She was going to be later than normal, still on time for the meeting. Lucas was pretty brave to call a meeting without conferring with her. This was all so ridiculous. If all the other things hadn't happened, she'd ignore the fluid and go onto work.

Chapter Seventeen

"What?" Colton shook his head. The minutes had ticked by slowly since he climbed into bed, and he had never hit deep sleep when his cell phone started ringing. Whoever it was, it better be good. His plans of sleeping all day were not coming to fruition.

"It's Brandon. Where are you right now?"

"At home. In bed. Where are you?"

"On my way to Brynleigh's."

"Why?" Colton sat up. Alarms sounded in his head. He'd been at her house for most of the night, arrived after dark and had left in the dark, just before the sun rose.

"You need to meet me over there. I know, I know. She's not your responsibility anymore. She told me."

Colton groaned.

"She said you quit."

"True. I couldn't seem to bring myself to work for the same corporation that is trying to destroy the ranch. You'd better watch out for your own ranch." Colton pulled on jeans and a hooded sweatshirt.

"We can talk about that later. It's Brynleigh I'm

concerned about right now. She thinks someone may have tampered with her car."

Colton paused. "I was there most of the night. It didn't happen on my watch."

"Is it possible someone tampered with it at work, and it didn't bust until she got home and let the car sit overnight?"

"I suppose. Did she say what it looked like?"

"Brownish in color and smelled like fish oil. Like if you broke open a fish oil tablet and spilled it in her driveway. A lot of it."

"That's brake fluid, then." Colton quickly laced up his boots, let Bandit out, and jumped in his truck. Any sleep was out of the question now. "I'm on my way."

"Meet you there."

~

Brynleigh watched as Brandon's truck pulled alongside her car. He'd made record time. Maybe she wouldn't be late.

She pointed at the stain that had now seeped into the concrete.

Brandon drug two fingers through the residue and brought them to his nose. Frowning, he looked back up the cul-de-sac. Brynleigh looked, too.

Colton's truck careened around the corner. Oh no. Brynleigh blew out a breath.

"I called him. I know what you said, but maybe he has the bigger picture."

Oh, he's got the bigger picture, alright. Brynleigh stepped closer to Brandon.

Maybe he could deflect Colton's attitude a little. Colton pulled to the curb. It didn't look like he'd slept in days. Which he probably hadn't, she reasoned, because he was sitting outside her house most nights. The tug of war in her brain was exhausting. The fact he'd returned to her house because he thought she might be in danger was encouraging and yet, he'd come at Brandon's request, not hers.

He didn't look angry now, just resigned to the fact that she still needed help. If he thought she was some weak female, she'd give him a piece of her mind. How was she supposed to know what to do with brake fluid leaking out from under her car?

"I didn't call you." She resisted the urge to stomp her foot. He made her knees weak, her heart speed up, and her attitude frosty. She wanted to punch him or hug him or… argh. Or everything all at once. He spun her insides out, sent mixed signals, and made her think about him so much, he threatened to invade every piece of her. She growled under her breath. He was infuriating, but she had bigger fish to fry. Like getting to work in time for that meeting. "Brandon, can you take me to work? There's an important meeting I need to prepare for, and this may have to wait."

Brandon swung his gaze to Colton, eyebrows raised.

"I'll take you. I can swing back by and talk to Brandon about this." Colton patted the hood of her car.

Not her first choice, but she'd suffer through if it meant she'd be there on time. With a long look at Brandon, she followed Colton to his truck. She caught a glimpse of a smile when she climbed into his truck in her heels and skirt.

No one spoke during the drive. Brynleigh let her thoughts drift as the outside whizzed by her window. Not her fault his property was in the line of fire or that things kept happening to her. Dangerous things. She clamped her lips shut, her jaw muscles tight.

After a stoic 'thank you', she made her way up to her office. Juliette met her there, her face an indicator this was not a good meeting.

"Are you invited to the meeting?" Brynleigh asked her.

"Yes."

Brynleigh nearly cursed when she entered the boardroom, and her mother was at the head of the table with Lucas to her right. Her mother had regained her throne. At least for this meeting. Lucas greeted them with a tight smile.

"Mother." Her mother looked terrible. Her skin was white and pasty, and she had a bluish tint underneath her eyes. When was the last time Brynleigh had checked in on her? She hadn't looked like death warmed over then. The treatments were not being kind to Celeste. At least she still had her hair, although it looked thinner, and Brynleigh could see her scalp in places. Celeste sat tall on her throne and despite her ailing health, Brynleigh knew better than to let her guard down.

Maybe she was being fired. Wouldn't that be perfect? Then she and Colton could… wishful thinking. But then she'd have no opportunity to turn the casino around and save the ranch. Not if she was no longer Acting President. If she was brave, she'd sit at the other end of the table as if she were the opposing queen. Not that brave, girl. She sat across from Lucas, Juliette by her side.

"Brynleigh." Celeste looked down her nose at her. "Let's get this started, shall we?"

Of course, your highness.

"Brynleigh, update us on the current projects please." Celeste spoke to the group.

"I think I'm better suited to share information with you." Lucas smiled at Celeste.

"Is that true, Brynleigh? After all this time, Lucas is more equipped to inform me of the corporation projects?"

"It hasn't been all that…"

"I believe so." Lucas cut her off.

She needed to get the upper hand or she was going to lose any ability to speak up.

"I can do it." She addressed Lucas. "I'm not sure why you called this meeting, but I can suspect why. I am perfectly capable of informing my mother on the projects. In fact, I see no reason for you to be here."

Lucas scoffed.

"Let's get right down in the weeds then, shall we?" Brynleigh resisted the urge to stand and present her case in front of the judge and jury. "The casino property is the one you're concerned with the most, correct?" Brynleigh hesitated long enough to hear Lucas sputter. "The one we drive past every time we're out and you say how much money you'll make on the property? Not the corporation, but you… how much money you will make."

Celeste looked at Lucas. "My corporation. It

will be good for you to remember that."

Brynleigh proceeded. "The people who own the property where the casino plans are currently located are good people."

Celeste held up her hand to stop Brynleigh's plea. "We don't operate for good people."

Lucas smirked.

"I'm aware." Brynleigh grimaced. "I think it can be a win-win situation for everyone involved if we turn the casino property to the east slightly. It would avoid the ranch having to sell and the land to the east is unoccupied and vacant, so it shouldn't be difficult to snap it up."

Celeste narrowed her eyes at Brynleigh. "Who lives on the ranch, these good people, that you're so concerned with?"

"Her boyfriend." Lucas laughed, humorlessly.

Brynleigh refrained from slapping him. "He is not my boyfriend. He and his brother own the ranch, and they are doing good things there. I don't see why it's necessary to boot them out if there are other options."

Lucas smiled ingeniously at her. She looked like a blubbering idiot. What appeal could she make to her mother? None.

"The casino has to face the north, not the east, for the traffic to flow correctly from the city. Anyone knows that." Lucas spread out a map on the boardroom table.

He'd brought solid ammunition with him. She'd only brought her emotions. Of course, the meeting had been unexpected, and she hadn't had time to prepare for the slaughter.

"Brynleigh, daughter of mine, we do not operate on kindness. We operate on facts and knowledge. I do believe you may be too close to the project. Lucas, I'm turning this over to you. Please draw up any papers you need to push this through, and let's get this project off the drawing room floor."

Brynleigh slumped in her seat. Her mother would never listen to her. And Colton would pay the price.

She followed Juliette back to her office. "These are good people doing good things. Apparently, Mother thinks I'm incapable of handling this project, and I think only with my heart and not my head."

Juliette turned to her. "Your heart?"

"Yeah, you know, for that ranch."

Really? The ranch? Or Colton?

~

"What do you think?" Colton knelt in the driveway next to Brandon, who was half under the car.

"It's definitely her brakes, bro."

"Cut? Or damaged?"

"I'd say sliced open. This looks pretty intentional." Brandon crawled out and leaned back against the car. "You have to call the cops."

"They've already been out here once. For the brick." Colton got out his cell phone. "There were only brief windows of time when I wasn't here. Before it got dark and just before daylight, I went home."

"Well, I guess it could have happened while she was at work. Maybe it was cut slightly and opened up when she pulled into the driveway. Either way, you've got to report it." Colton gave him a hand up. "That's like three things in a row that have threatened her safety."

"I know. And I just resigned."

He should have… no, no way. He couldn't have stayed on knowing they wanted to take the ranch. It wasn't just a conflict of interest. This is where he lived. Where his brother had established something good in a spot that held so much bad. And how long had Brynleigh known? When was she going to tell him? He had feelings for her, she knew that. Maybe she was just being nice, suckering him in until she dropped the bomb. Maybe she thought he would give in if she were the one asking. He really didn't know her. His comment had been a low blow, but what if he'd been right? What if it really was all about the money?

And all of the times he'd come to her rescue? She appeared grateful, if not a little obnoxious about the whole superhero thing. His gut told him she'd been honest about her feelings, but he'd been wrong before when feelings got in the picture.

"You calling the cops or am I?" Brandon waved him back to the present.

"You call. I'll text Brynleigh."

Brandon says your brakes were cut. Calling the police now.

You've got to be kidding. Why? I haven't done anything to anyone. Tell me why. Nvm. Send them to me when they're done with u.

Do you need a ride home?

No. No longer your responsibility. She was using his words against him. He may have said them, but…well… a little different scenario when her life was on the line.

Chapter Eighteen

Brynleigh shook her head. An exhausting day in a string of exhausting days. First, with her car and Brandon calling Colton, then with her mother and Lucas, back to the car with the police, and now Colton's truck was sitting outside her house again. Brynleigh looked over at Juliette in the driver's seat of Juliette's car.

"Did you call him?" She exhaled.

Juliette nodded as she pulled into the driveway.

The wind whipped the treetops around them, blowing leaves across the windshield. The newscasters warned of thunderstorms heading their way with tornadic possibilities. Brynleigh had called it a day and asked Juliette to take her home. Maybe a good storm would blow her rough edges down into the Gulf of Mexico. Not likely. If she were lucky, she'd get some hot tea, a bubble bath, and a good book to read. Maybe not in that order, especially if she were forced to the basement due to the severe weather. Maybe a tornado would pick her up and drop her on a bad witch at the start of a yellow brick road. She didn't need the wizard, though. Waking up in a different land would suffice.

"Why?" Brynleigh huffed. "I told him I didn't need him. I can't save his ranch. He wants nothing to do with me."

"The police report indicates you do. The brick through your window says you do. Your cut brakes say you do. You need protection until we figure this out."

"Juliette, you've become such a good friend to me in such a short time, but from now on, please leave him," Brynleigh pointed at Colton's truck, "out of my business."

Rain began to drop in earnest as the wind picked up speed.

"Are you going to be okay going home?"

"I will be. I need to go now, though."

"Ok, I'll call you later. Text me when you're home." Brynleigh dashed for her front door. Her foot glanced off a wet brick and she fell to the ground. Brynleigh sat up, rain pelting her body. Her ankle was on fire, despite the freezing, whipping rain. No way could she stand. She'd have to scoot on her rear end up the steps, at least until she was under the covered doorstep. She looked towards Colton's truck. He ran toward her, wind tearing at his hair.

Colton picked her up as if she were a tiny doll and cradled her in his arms. She stuck her hand in her pocket and searched for the house keys. Of course, they were in the other pocket. He swiped them from her.

He unlocked the door and stepped into the foyer. She didn't want to leave the safety of his arms, but they were puddling on the floor.

"Can you put any weight on it?"

Gently, she put her foot down, but yelped when the pain shot up her leg. "No, can you help me to the kitchen? We can puddle safer there without ruining my floors."

Colton let her lean on him and pulled out a kitchen chair for her to sit on.

"Where are your towels?" He started down the hall.

"Second door to your left. In the bathroom."

Brynleigh could see the footprints he made on the floors and grimaced. She'd have to clean them later. Colton brought out two towels for her and one for himself. Taking his shoes off at the door, he pulled paper towels off the roll and wiped up his wet footprints.

That was considerate.

She wound one of the fluffy towels around her hair, stacking it on top of her head. He handed the other one to her.

"I'm going to have to get out of these clothes." She almost smiled at his uncomfortable look.

"Um… yeah."

"Can you help me to my bedroom? I can change in there. I might have some clothes that fit you."

"I'll get you settled, and then I'll head home."

"Ok." Brynleigh put her arm around his neck and leaned her weight on him. He smelled good, like wet soap, and she resisted the urge to lean in further. Always the hero, she wouldn't be able to return the kindness by saving his ranch. Brynleigh felt moisture drip down her face and knew it wasn't from her hair. "This is good, thanks."

Brynleigh pulled open a drawer on her dresser. Old painting shirts and shorts were all she had. "Will this do?"

Colton looked at the clothes in her hand and grinned. A grin that almost undid her. The pink splotched painting shirt and white shorts didn't suit him?

"It's all I got." She smiled back.

Colton covered his grin with his hand, and his voice took on a serious tone. "I'll take them, but I really am going home after you get changed and settled."

"Ok." Brynleigh looked at the floor. If he'd only stay longer.

~

Colton stepped back into the kitchen. He'd just stand on the tile until she called for his help, and then he'd put his wet boots back on and race for home. Once she was settled in a chair and after he'd assessed her ankle, he'd be on his way.

It was probably a sprained ankle. He rubbed his hand across the stubble on his cheek. Looking around the brightly decorated kitchen, with its red walls and pot of sunflowers on the table, he could see her effectively burning down the house. He chuckled. When he'd cooked dinner for her in her own kitchen, he thought the space was well-equipped and sunny, large enough for two to cook, or at least putter. She was clearly not a cook, despite her wide range of utensils and equipment. He guessed they were part of the decor as she said she often had carry out or delivery. While he was waiting, he could put on a cup of tea for her. Colton debated. Was that too nice for the lady he wanted to strangle? For the person he wanted to keep on holding in his arms until nothing else mattered? He shook himself. What the heck? He needed to stay focused on the goal. What was the goal again? Keep the farm. Maybe his kindness would help her change her mind on the ranch. Wouldn't that be manipulation? Wasn't that what she was doing? She probably had nothing to do with the sale of the ranch. She said she wasn't even in position as acting president when the idea of the casino was first developed. She'd just lost her bookstore when they met, and he was the night watchman. Those were simpler times. Now, he stood contemplating being nice and fixing her a cup of tea. On the other hand, she could be scheming behind his back. Couldn't there be a happy medium? Why did it have to swing so far to the left or right? Either she was totally naive about the whole process or she was one very good conniver. He should just leave.

Colton moved over to the large new window. Rain was coming in sheets now. Good thing he was already wet. He'd only make it two steps outside before he'd be soaked again. He watched as a trashcan blew down the road.

The lights flickered. No, no, no. Please don't let the lights go out.

As if the powers that be heard and ignored him, the lights flickered one more time and then he stood in pitch darkness. Only the lightning outside illuminated the room in brief spurts.

"Colton?" Brynleigh's small voice echoed down the hall.

"I'm still here. Do you need help?" Colton

could hear her hopping down the hallway, shoulder against the wall. He stood still so she could see him when the next lightning bolt hit.

"I think I got it." She plopped onto the couch. "I don't think you can drive in this weather."

Nope.

"You want to see if you can fit in those clothes I gave you?"

Nope. He couldn't stand in the kitchen on the tile floor though, either. He was already chilled from the dampness.

"I don't think I have a choice at this point." He took one last glance at the sheets of rain hitting the window, scooped up the clothes, and went into the bathroom. God, why are you doing this to me? I don't want to be here. That's a lie. He did want to be with Brynleigh, but he didn't want to be in these circumstances.

The T-shirt she had given him fit fine, although the shorts were a little short. Still, they were better than wet jeans and dripping flannel.

"Good thing you can't see me."

"I bet you're always cute."

Colton raised his eyebrows. Was she flirting? Her ankle must not be hurting too bad. He had to be on guard. His ranch may depend on how he treated her.

"I'm coming over to you. I want to check your ankle, make sure it isn't broken." Colton sat down next to her. She put her leg in his lap. He closed his eyes. Focus, Colton. He couldn't see her leg, but he could feel the shapely length of it and the muscle in her calf. Smooth and soft to the touch, he used both hands to move down to her ankle.

"You're shivering. Do you want a blanket?" He stopped his inspection.

"Um, yeah. I'm shivering. And yes, a blanket would be nice."

Colton flipped on his phone light and spotted a fluffy white blanket in a basket by the chair. "That one?" He followed where she pointed.

"Yes, that will work."

Colton carefully propped her ankle up and retrieved the blanket. Tucking it around her, he came close to her face. So close he could… back away now. He scooted back into the spot he'd vacated and took her foot back into his hands. She shivered again. Was she going into shock? Colton racked his brain for any useful medical knowledge he had for shock patients.

"Are you still cold?"

"Colton, I'm not cold." Brynleigh leaned toward him. "You have my foot in your hands. It's not every day I find my foot in a superhero's hands. Usually, my foot is in *my* mouth."

Colton released the breath he was holding. So, she wasn't cold. His touch made her shiver. And the superhero part? No way. He ran his hands down the inside of her ankle and manipulated it to the left and right. She groaned at the movement. The swelling had escalated.

"It's not broken, but it may be sprained. Do you have any frozen peas or frozen water bottles to put on it?" He moved away from her. Crazy that a touch could tell more than words. So naive with women. This was going to be a long night. Lord, help him.

"You can see what I've got in the freezer." She pointed to the part freezer, part fridge.

"I don't want to keep the door open long in case the lights are off for a while."

"I know."

Colton came back with an ice pack wrapped in a kitchen towel. "Perfect." He started to sit in the chair opposite from her, distance he needed, but she stopped him.

"Please. Sit over here."

Colton sat down next to her against his better judgment.

"Can we just talk?"

"No, not about Texas A&D. About you, yes, and why these things keep happening."

Brynleigh scooted closer to him and threw part of the blanket over his knees. Its warmth was surprising, and he pulled it up further. All he had to do was move his arm over her head, and she'd be tucked in nice and snug. He could feel her body heat through his T-shirt. His thoughts muddled. What was he saying? Oh right, they could talk all they wanted about her and the danger, but nothing about the job.

"Juliette is concerned. So am I." Not really about the job. "I think we have to assume that I'm a target for someone. Who, though? And why? What have I done?"

Colton shook his head. "I don't know, but it started way back with the fire."

"Before then. I had already called 911 before the fire."

"True. I don't really know what to think. What did the police say?"

"Not much. Then they were called out about the car, had it hauled away as evidence. Said they'd be in contact about what I wanted to do with it afterwards, like which mechanic shop to send it to. I cannot believe all of this is happening. Colton?" Brynleigh touched his cheek and ran the backside of her hand down his whiskers.

Nope. Nope. Nope.

Colton caught her hand. "Brynleigh, I… well, I…" He couldn't seem to spit the words out. Before he could retract his action, he kissed her palm. Her shiver next to him was tell-tale. "Brynleigh," he started again. "I'm going to be honest with you. This will never work."

Brynleigh wiggled her hand free and put it on his chest. Surely, she could feel the rhythm his heart was tattooing loudly. "Why not?"

"Why not?" Why not, indeed. What was the reasoning again? It was like her touch caused all the brains to fall out of his head. He turned to face her. Big mistake, she was inches from him. "Listen, maybe in another time or space, but not.."

Brynleigh kissed him. The old Meatloaf song lyrics 'She took the words right outta my mouth' floated through his head. While in Rome… Colton kissed her back. Light, quick kisses, and Colton struggled to breathe. His heart raced. He had to get out ahead of this runaway train before it jumped the tracks and caused irreparable damage. Colton moved his hands away from her face and down to her shoulders. Pushing her back into the cushions, he stood up, knocking the blanket to the floor. Silence settled in the room. "I'm sorry."

"I'm not." Brynleigh retrieved the blanket. "That's been building for a while now."

True. He wouldn't acknowledge that to her, though. He settled back into a chair across the room. She stretched out on the couch, and soon he could hear her soft snores. Glad someone was able to sleep. He knew it wouldn't be him. Not tonight, maybe not for a while. Not with the memory of those kisses riding roughshod on his heart.

Chapter Nineteen

"Brynleigh, sorry I didn't call when I got home. That storm was ferocious. Did Colton's truck hold up out by the curb? I see it's gone now." Juliette stood at her front door.

"Thanks for picking me up. I'm surprised there's not more damage out here." Brynleigh hesitated to place her foot on the brick walk.

"Oh, my goodness, what happened?"

Brynleigh grimaced. Brynleigh lifted her pant leg to expose the bandage wrapped around her ankle. She couldn't slide anything past her friend.

"I tripped on the walkway last night. Colton brought me in."

Juliette looked sideways at her. "So, he didn't ride out the storm in his truck."

Not much a question, but rather a statement.

"Um, no. He stayed inside."

"Really. I'm surprised you two are still alive, all cooped up in the house together." Juliette stopped at Brynleigh's tone. "Oh. Apparently, very much alive."

"Stop it. We talked and that was it."

"Using your words, and since we're such good

friends now," Juliette got in the driver's seat, "why would you lie to me?"

Brynleigh turned pink. She clearly could not lie. She'd kissed him first, which had set off a series of kisses, each more passionate than the last, until he'd nearly jumped off the couch. For the best, if she were honest. His mind was probably ticking off the ways she'd tried to manipulate him. Little did he know how far her heart was engaged. She did not, however, have control over the casino deal, try as she might.

Juliette scoffed at her silence.

"Can we just get to work?" Brynleigh lightly punched her new friend.

"I'm still a little concerned, though. I don't think anything bad will happen to you at work, but if Colton is off the job, there's no one at home to protect you."

"Colton and I talked a little about that this morning," Brynleigh cleared her throat. "If I'm off the project, is there any reason for me to still be concerned?"

"Well, if the casino deal was the motivating factor for all of this, I'd say no, but you're still acting president. If that's the motivating factor, then yes. I think you need to be really careful."

"You think this all has something to do with Texas A&D? And maybe not me personally?"

"Girl, you *are* Texas A&D right now. And I do think it's all connected."

Brynleigh digested the information for a minute. "Juliette, how long have you worked with Lucas?"

"About five years. You think he may be behind this?"

"I'm just voicing my thoughts. I am not crazy about him."

"He's pretty cutthroat, but so is your mother, which makes them perfect partners. And the casino is his baby."

Juliette turned into the garage and shut off the engine.

"Do you need help?"

"No, but thank you. Once I get in my office, I'll prop my ankle up and get some of the weight off it. I'll be fine."

In the hallway, they separated, and Brynleigh unlocked her office door. She limped over to the desk and plopped into the chair with a groan. Colton had been certain she only had a sprain, and ice and pain relievers would do the trick. She couldn't resist the indulgence of remembering her foot in the palm of his hand. She'd felt safe, as always, with him.

In the center of her desk was a large envelope with her name scrawled across it. Opening the package, several documents fell out with 'COPIES' stamped on them. Colton and Mark's ranch, legal documents, maps, and architect drawings were included.

Brynleigh flipped through the documents and cried out at the signature on the last one, Celeste Tavish. Not only had her mother taken her off the project, but she'd also signed documents that started the legal process of purchasing the property. Colton would truly hate her now.

~

Colton drove slowly home and pulled into the area next to his house. He had managed to dry his clothes in Brynleigh's dryer while she slept, and the clothes she'd loaned him were sitting in a bag next to him. He'd throw them in the laundry before returning them to her.

Colton's mind turned over with possibilities. He had no job, the ranch was being pursued by Texas A&D as their next great adventure, and the woman he was beginning to really care about was being threatened. Ironic that she was also the head of Texas A&D, but couldn't figure out a way to stop the casino. This was truly a mess.

Hey God, Big Guy in the Sky, whatever you are to Mark, couldn't you just swoop down and reset all of the playing pieces, please? Maybe God wasn't interested in them staying on the ranch, either. Colton couldn't imagine any other place to call home, though. Despite the bad memories, what his brother was doing now was good. He should be allowed to continue doing good with the boys. Maybe he was the one bringing the destruction to the ranch. Maybe God would throw out Mark and his selfless work with the juveniles because Colton was bad. Wouldn't that be rich? Everywhere he went, he left damaged people, animals, things in his wake.

After a shower, Colton walked around the half acre, picking up sticks and things overturned by the storm. He should be sleeping since he hadn't last night. Watching Brynleigh relax and sleep had been bittersweet. Her slight snores were music to his ears, and he didn't want to shut his eyes for a minute at the risk of falling to sleep and missing out on the sight and sound of her. He knew if he laid down today, he'd lie awake with that vision in his head and not be able to rest. Better to do something physical and exhausting than lay in bed daydreaming of possibilities that could never happen. Plus, if he was truly bad and God was punishing him for being a screw up, Brynleigh was in that path of destruction, too. Back on that merry-go-round. He loved being around her, she drove him crazy both physically and emotionally. Then, she'd do something, or allow something to happen, and he was mad and wanted nothing to do with her. Another dip in the ride and someone did something to her and she needed protection and they were right back at the start of the ride. But if God was the attendant, letting people on and off, would He stop the ride and make her get off, along with Mark and the boys? Leave him spinning in the air like a broken amusement ride?

Brandon's truck pulled into the drive around lunchtime.

"Checkin' in on you all." Brandon waved at him.

"We made it through without too much damage." Colton shook his hand.

"And Brynleigh?"

"What about her?" Colton looked sharply at Brandon. Of course, he'd be interested in how she was doing after the cut brakes. He knew nothing about Colton staying the night inside the house.

"Um…just wondering."

"Sorry. My head's spinning with everything that's happened." Colton offered a lame excuse. He hopped up on the tailgate of his truck, half full with branches and sticks he'd picked up. Brandon sat with him. "I'm assuming you know about Texas A&D wanting this ranch to build a casino. They want to bulldoze the property to make way for progress."

Brandon snorted. "I heard. They talked to us, too, since the western town sits so close to what they are wanting to do. It's kinda scary when the person you care about is being targeted."

Colton frowned. "Are we still talking about the ranch?"

"When you said everything, I assumed you included Brynleigh in that statement. Am I wrong?"

Colton squirmed. Were his thoughts about Brynleigh when he'd said 'everything'? Texas A&D? Or a wider scope, like him in general, buckled in on that merry-go-round? "I think it's a little more than that, but yes, Brynleigh, too, I suppose."

"I know you've heard some of this, but when I was undercover at the prison, Selena was in a lot of trouble. She was coerced and blackmailed into doing something illegal to save her father. She got caught." Brandon paused. "Fortunately, or rather God, allowed me to be in a position where I could see the whole picture and bail her out when the time came to do so."

"That's quite a story. But God? Honestly? You think He allowed that? Why would He do that? Why not just make things happen differently, if He's in control, so she wasn't in that situation in the first place?" Colton knew parts of Brandon's story, but none of Selena's. So far neither Colton nor Brynleigh had done anything illegal that he knew of. The corner of his lips tightened. That he knew of. Why did God come up in every conversation these days?

"It was pretty tough to sit and watch it all unfold and not do anything about it. She was emotionally targeted by her boss, blackmailed by the guy she was seeing, and harassed by inmates. It was ugly." Brandon turned towards Colton. "I know you want to protect her. And I know you have feelings for her. That's evident every time you'all are together. You'll have to sort that out. But the God questions? Colton, God is so much different than you perceive Him. I don't know what your father was like, but the comparison is rarely close to what the Big Guy is like. He does have control, but He loves us enough to let us have free will, too. He wants us to choose Him, but if we don't, then He allows us to do what we want. He didn't make robots."

"That's a lot."

"I know. It just spills out when I get to tell others how amazing God is."

"Back to Brynleigh. She can do something about this situation. She's not being coerced or blackmailed. She's choosing not to."

"You sure about that?"

"She's the acting president. She can do whatever she wants."

"It sounds like there is someone who is not very happy with her, though. Maybe there's pressure you know nothing about. Or a plan."

"Well, I can't do anything now. I quit. I can't work for a woman who wants to bulldoze my land for a casino. And as far as a plan goes, I'm assuming you're talking about God again. How would this benefit Him? Or her, to be honest?"

"We don't often know God's plans until they've completely unfolded and it's in our hindsight. I suspect if we did know His plans, we'd run screaming into the night. That's the freedom in knowing He's in control, and we have to trust His plan is good."

Colton stared off into the distance and sighed. It appeared he and God were going to have a serious conversation soon. What Brandon said did not equate with how Colton thought about God.

"When did you quit? Before or after her brakes got cut?" Brandon leaned back on the tailgate.

"Before. But then I stayed the night last night." Colton let slip.

"Whoa, you did what?" Brandon jumped to the ground.

"Not like that. I couldn't just leave her unprotected at the house, so I went and sat outside."

"Oh, sorry. I shouldn't have reacted so strongly. I just see the fireworks with you guys and was concerned that..." Brandon sat back down on the tailgate.

Colton raised his eyebrows.

"Come on, dude. There were always sparks flying off both of you." Brandon explained.

"Interesting. She fell outside on the slippery brick and then the storm chased me inside." Colton grimaced. That sounded lame.

"The storm chased you inside? Really?"

"Yeah, sounds bad even to my ears."

"Look, I know how tempting this can be."

"It's not as tempting as you think. There can never be a way Brynleigh and I can have anything together. She wants to build a casino on my property. End of story. There's no way."

"Your property?" Colton and Brandon looked over their shoulder to see Mark standing by the truck.

"Well, and yours." Colton bit the inside of his cheek. It really wasn't all his. The deed had both boys' names on it.

"Colton, I've been thinking," Mark started.

Colton shook his head.

"Listen, hear me out." Mark pointed beyond the barn. "There's thirty acres that way we could sell off. What if we kept the property these houses sit on and some acreage for the goats?"

"Seriously? The goats?" Colton rolled his eyes. The goats could go, too, for all he cared.

"And the horses."

"What about the cattle? You just want to get rid of them, too?"

"The Lord works in mysterious ways, my friend." Brandon muttered.

Colton's gaze swung between his obviously loco brother to his new friend.

"What?"

"I wanted to check on you all after the storm, but I also wanted to let you know some of your cattle escaped through the fence and ended up in our pasture. Guess the storm spooked them."

"So? We'll come get them."

"When I was telling Selena and her pa about the cattle, I had a bright idea. I suspect it was from God, but I'm just guessing. Thought I'd run it by you this morning."

Colton's chest heaved. There were changes

coming and none of them he had anticipated. Another God-plan he knew nothing about? Colton scoffed.

"Every time we have a rodeo or event where we're borrowing your cattle, you have to drive them over to our place. You aren't using them for anything else, are you? Beef?"

"No. Occasionally, we slaughter one for meat, but only occasionally." Mark shook his head.

"What if we just kept them over at our ranch, used them when we needed, and paid for their vet bills and such?"

"How does that benefit anyone?" Colton questioned.

Brandon pointed out beyond the barn where they could see cattle lying down in the pasture or standing, eating at the round bales of hay. Exactly where Mark had pointed.

Understanding dawned. If they could convince Texas A&D to take a portion of their land and not the whole thing, then it was a win-win situation. And if they drew up the casino's drawings to face away from the ranch, maybe, just maybe, it would be okay. Maybe he had plans, too, and wouldn't wait for God.

"It's worth a thought."

"Dude, now you can go be the hero again. Claim your prize. Woo the princess." Brandon nudged Colton with his elbow.

Colton smirked. Maybe he'd do just that. Convincing Brynleigh would be the next hurdle.

Chapter Twenty

Her mother had done it again. Run roughshod over her. It was as if Celeste held a plan book and knew two steps before she did. When she'd stepped away from the president position and coerced Brynleigh into temporarily taking her spot, she knew Brynleigh would feel obligated to do her bidding, because she was sick, and because she dangled the new bookstore in front of her. Did she really just trade this mess for a new business? Would her mother follow through with her promise? When she accepted the position with reservation and the prize, did her mother see her as a sappy, little girl who could be manipulated?

It was no use. If she did anything her mother didn't like, Celeste would take back the reins and do what she wanted. Brynleigh would never be a part of this cutthroat world. Nor did she want to. She wanted to be involved in the community. She wanted to help people be better versions of themselves. Celeste was all about the power and almighty dollar. Brynleigh doubted her mother even noticed the people she destroyed. Only the things that glittered mattered.

How did God make totally different people,

family? Her mother was motivated only by greed. Brynleigh wanted personal relationships. Celeste manipulated and coerced. Brynleigh encouraged and built people up. Selena was always mentioning God, but if He had anything to do with this, He'd certainly messed up.

The sermon at Selena and Brandon's church came to mind. Love was not conditional, or rude, or self-serving. Maybe, just maybe, her mother's love wasn't truly love at all.

She'd been running away from her mother's influence for so long and yet, she caved as soon as her mother offered a trade, her bidding for a new bookstore. That's what her mother did to get her way. Brynleigh had seen the opportunity to get what she wanted and had been a willing participant in the manipulation.

Ugh. This was a vicious circle and not one she could easily break. It was her mother, for Pete's sake, and maybe she really wasn't well enough to continue at the moment. She had not looked well at the meeting. What would her mother be like if not in control? She couldn't imagine Celeste being anything other than powerful. Certainly not sickly. She'd always known her mother to take charge, manipulate if necessary, and bring her A game to every situation. What if her mother thought she was losing control? Of her health? Her empire? Her reputation? How would she react? Be devastated… and manic… and desperate. Her mother was always going to step in and take projects back to retain control if Brynleigh didn't do what she asked. But what if she became too ill to do so? Would Brynleigh have to lead the corporation indefinitely? And never see a new bookstore? That wasn't something she wanted to dwell on.

Or she could quit now. Get out. Find a way to help the community, do what she loved. She wouldn't be able to help Colton, not that she'd ever been able to turn that horse around. The casino on his property had been established before she'd arrived on the scene.

Brynleigh blew hair out of her face. She had no idea what to do. Her ankle burned, her head hurt, and her heart was attached to a man that could never be hers.

He'd always managed to show up and be her hero through the fire, the brick, and the cut brakes. And when she had the opportunity to reciprocate, she couldn't pull it off. He'd been so mad, and yet, still obligated to protect her. Maybe that wasn't right. She felt obligated to her mother, but maybe Colton had other reasons. Different reasons. Like what the pastor said, love doesn't hold grudges. Could they repair their friendship, and maybe more, if Brynleigh stepped down from Texas A&D? Was that a pipedream?

She couldn't step away for Colton, though. It had to be for her. Staying at Texas A&D long term would be the death of her spirit, especially if Celeste had the ability to waltz in anytime she wanted to. If she was going to quit, she had to do it for herself.

Brynleigh's phone rang. Colton's name showed on the ID. Did her thoughts conjure up the phone call? Brynleigh snorted. Hardly.

"Hello?"

"Hey, how are you?"

Not the question she was expecting. She hadn't really expected to hear from him ever again after leaving her house this morning.

"Fine, my ankle's still swollen and hurts like crazy, but I'm fine."

"Take some aspirin and call me in the morning."

Brynleigh looked again at the caller ID. The person on the other line sounded way too chipper to be the Colton she knew.

"I'm kidding. I've got something I want to run by you. Are you at the office?"

"Yes, but–"

"Okay, I'll be there in about a half an hour."

He hung up before she could tell him it was no use. Celeste had already signed the papers that would officially destroy his ranch.

~

If this worked, selling a portion of the land, not only would the ranch remain intact, but he and Brynleigh could potentially see each other on a formal basis. That's what he wanted, right? His heart said yes.

Brynleigh was being manipulated by Texas A&D, in the form of Celeste Tavish or Lucas. Surely, she recognized that.

Colton drove his truck into the guest parking lot and greeted the security guard. Apparently, the word was not out yet about his resignation.

"Doing okay, George?" Wouldn't hurt to be friendly with the guy.

"Doing just fine, Mr. Bruens."

Out of the corner of his eye, Colton noticed a disheveled man in street clothes approach the security gate. Moving behind George, Colton crossed his arms and took a better look at the guy. The man appeared to be drunk and had a sign Colton couldn't read in his hand. He noticed Lucas come in from a side door and turn toward the elevators.

"There he is. That's the man who stole my land," the man yelled and jumped through the gate. Startled, George attempted to stop him, but was shoved to the floor.

"You okay, George?" Noting the nod, Colton went after the man who was sprinting towards Lucas. All of the drunken stupor was gone.

Colton yelled at Lucas, who stopped just as the man collided into him.

"What?" Lucas toppled to the ground.

Colton reached the two when he saw the flash of a steel blade. Colton grabbed the man's coat and hauled him backwards. The man howled and lunged at Colton. The two wrestled until Colton knocked the knife out of his hand. Flipping him over, Colton held his hands behind his back.

"George? You got cuffs?"

"Yes, sir. Never had to use them before." George handed them to Colton.

"Well, today's your lucky day." Colton sat the man up after securing the cuffs. "Call PD and have them come get him. Disorderly conduct." Colton looked around for the knife. "Change that to assault."

"Will do."

"Lucas, you okay?"

Lucas stood outside the elevator door, frozen.

"Lucas?"

"Yes, sorry. I've never been attacked like that." Lucas looked shell-shocked. "Thanks."

"Got here at the right time. Mind if I ride up with you?"

"Sure." Lucas continued to stare at Colton. Colton reached around him and pushed the up button.

"Helps if you push the button."

"You've got a little–" Lucas motioned to his nose.

Colton swiped his hand across his face. His hand came away with traces of blood. When the elevator dinged on their floor, Colton and Lucas went separate ways down the hall.

Stopping halfway, Colton turned and walked back to Lucas. "Mind if I check my face in your bathroom? I came up to talk to Brynleigh, but I don't want to show up with blood on my face. Women, you know?"

"Of course." Lucas unlocked his office door. "Thanks again. I really didn't know what was happening. I mean, we hired security for that reason, but to my knowledge, it's never happened before."

Colton glanced at Lucas, who chewed on a fingernail, still visibly shaking.

The adrenaline rush slowed down, and Colton looked around the office. Lucas had never been supportive of Brynleigh, and his gut reaction told him Lucas may be behind some of the threats. Was he vindictive enough to start a fire? Cut her brakes? If so, he'd just stepped into the lion's den. An enemy of Brynleigh was an enemy of his. The hairs on the back of his neck stood up.

Colton closed the door to the narrow bathroom and looked at himself in the mirror. The split on his nose had reopened, and there were traces of blood on one side of his nose. He looked as disheveled as the attacker downstairs as he ran fingers through his hair. Grabbing a towel from the towel bar, Colton thanked whoever the bathroom designer was for the black hand towels. He would have made a mess of white towels. He wiped at the blood and then washed the blood off the towel.

Spotting a dot of blood on the floor, Colton looked under the sink for cleaning supplies. A Clorox wipe would do. Nothing but toilet paper and soap. He opened the cabinet doors and found what he was looking for. As he pulled out the Clorox wipe container, he knocked over a small basket full of odds and ends. Colton grimaced as he knelt to retrieve the items and restore them to their spot.

A paperclip, some pennies, and a glass bee.

Colton turned the glass over in the palm of his hand. Too small to be anything much, it caught the light and sent rainbow prisms around the small room.

"Everything okay in there?" Lucas knocked on the door.

"Yeah, just opened up an old wound. I'll be out in a second." Colton lied.

The bee looked familiar. Colton looked closer at the line tied to the bee. Fishing line. What the heck? Brynleigh had glass bees hanging in the window of her bookstore. The ones left after the fire had swayed in the breeze when they entered, catching his eye. How did Lucas have a glass bee from Brynleigh's bookstore? Unless… he'd been in her bookstore. Maybe the night of the fire. Which meant he could be the one who started the fire.

Colton tucked the bee in his pocket and stepped out of the bathroom. Lucas watched him. He was certain about the bee, but he'd confirm with Brynleigh before talking with the police.

Colton cautiously walked down the hallway. He had to be discreet. Brynleigh wasn't in her office. He strode to Juliette's office. "Juliette, where's Brynleigh?"

"She went downstairs. She heard there was some kind of scuffle at security." Juliette followed him back into the hallway.

Colton looked down at his shirt where he'd stashed the bee and froze. Lucas had to have seen it, too. The fishing wire attached to the bee had sprung from his pocket and was now visible. He knew. Lucas knew what Colton had taken from his bathroom. Colton punched the elevator buttons. He had to get to Brynleigh. Lucas had not left his office, so there was still time.

In the lobby, George was still talking to the police officer, who had arrived to pick up the assaulter. Brynleigh listened in on the conversation. To her he whispered, "Meet me by my truck. It's in the visitors' lot. I'll explain later."

"Okay." Brynleigh separated from the conversation and started toward the parking area.

Colton glanced over his shoulder. He could see the lights on the elevator descending. Lucas was on his way down. He stepped out into the sunshine just as the elevator doors opened.

He hurried to the truck and slid into the driver's

seat. "Give me a minute to get out of the area, and I'll show you what I found."

Brynleigh was silent, glancing at him from time to time as they made their way out of the city.

"What in the world is happening?" She turned to him as they stopped in a grocery parking lot. Random people were loading groceries in and out of their cars, not interested in the dirty pickup.

"Does this look familiar?" Colton pulled the end of the fishing wire out of his pocket. The bee fell out into the palm of his hand.

Brynleigh carefully picked it up and held it up to the window. The prisms sent rainbows dancing around the truck. "Yes, it hung in my store with several others. Where did you find it?"

Colton sighed. "In Lucas' bathroom."

"Why? Why would he have it? How did he get it in the first place?" Tears began to run down her face. "Are you saying…"

"That he may have been in your store during the break in and fire?" Colton reached over and took her hand in his. Her fingers were ice cold. "I can't imagine he would be doing the dirty work. Maybe whoever was working for him. They might have grabbed it as a souvenir."

"Why? Why me? Why is all of this happening? I am so tired."

"I think your mom set this up."

"The fire? She's mean, but not like this."

"No, I mean she knew Lucas thought he was next in line to take over the throne, and she knew he'd be furious when she named you at that gala."

"If he's behind the fire and break in, he knew

about me long before the gala."

"True." Colton stroked her palm with his thumb. "Let's go tell the police and then get you somewhere safe."

Brynleigh sniffed. "The only place I truly feel safe is with you."

Colton groaned. He was not a superhero. What if he couldn't keep her safe?

Chapter 20

When they reached the police station, Colton helped her out of the truck.

"How's your ankle?" Colton held her as he swung the door shut. She suspected he would carry her in if she needed it.

"I can walk, Colton."

"I know, I know. I keep thinking Lucas is going to turn up at every corner, and it's important the police know as soon as possible. I think Lucas knows what I found." Colton explained about the fishing wire sticking out of his pocket. "Pretty stupid to keep such damaging evidence at your place of work."

"He's arrogant enough to keep it there, though."

Brynleigh and Colton sat down with a detective and told them what they knew.

"So, what you're saying is all of these things are connected to Texas A&D and you." The detective pointed his pen at Brynleigh. "The store fire, the cut brakes, the glass bee."

"Yes." Colton answered for her.

"Look, if you're not connected to this… situation directly, why don't you wait out in the lobby?"

"This investigation, you mean? I'm her security." Colton put an arm around the back of Brynleigh's chair.

"I can see that."

"What he means is," Brynleigh glared at Colton. "He is my personal security guard at work. Texas A&D. Or was."

"Personal? Was? And who are you to Texas A&D?"

This was turning into a royal circus complete with clowns and acrobatics.

"Colton, would you please go sit in the lobby?" She needed this detective to take her seriously and he obviously couldn't with Colton speaking for her and confounding the situation.

Colton stood up from his chair, locking eyes with the detective. He strode from the room without any additional comments.

"Let me start from the beginning." Brynleigh laid out all of the details from when she called 911 to the present.

"Well, that sounds like a Hollywood movie." The detective leaned back in his chair. "Leave the evidence with me. I'll check the other reports and get back with you."

Brynleigh pulled the glass bee out of her pocket and sat it on the table between them. "It'll have both mine and Colton's prints on it. We both touched it."

"Of course. Just adds to the mystery." The detective snarled and escorted her back to the waiting room.

Colton wouldn't look at her.

"They are going to call me." Brynleigh sighed.

"I guess I will go back to work and act normal."

"Are you kidding me?" Colton jumped up and then ran fingers through his hair.

"What do you expect me to do? Where should I go? Hey, hero-man, where should I go?" How dare he question her every move as if she couldn't handle things for herself. Lucas didn't know she knew what Colton had found.

"I thought we agreed you'd go somewhere safe? You don't even have a car at the office if you needed one. You'd be a sitting duck." Colton distanced himself from her. "Will you please let me take you to Brandon and Selena's for the rest of the day?"

"Fine, but I can't hang out there forever." Brynleigh wouldn't let him help her into the truck. "You know none of this is my fault, and I'm sorry I couldn't do what you wanted. My mother signed all of the papers for the takeover, and there's nothing I can do."

Colton turned around and looked at her. She wanted to cringe under his gaze, but she kept her spine stiff and refused to meet his eyes. If she did, she'd dissolve into a puddle.

"And you always do what your mother wants you to do," Colton muttered.

"I'm sorry, can you say that a little louder?" Brynleigh shouted at him. Coward. He really did not know her at all. He was acting just like her mother… no trust… blaming her for things out of her control. "What you're saying is I did all of these things to get attention and even though you've saved me multiple times, I'm not willing to save your ranch. Is that what you're saying?"

"I'm saying everything is conditional with you. I save you," he put quotes in the air with his fingers. "You have to save me back or the score is uneven. Honestly, I don't know what you've done to help me save the ranch. I'm going to drop you by Brandon's, and then I'm off this merry-go-round. I resigned, thankfully, and I'm done."

"Yes, please do that." Brynleigh crossed her arms and stared out the window.

~

Brandon and Selena were both home when Colton knocked on their door. Brynleigh stood behind him, looking for all the world like she wanted to take him out. She was the most infuriating female he'd ever gotten involved with. He had split personalities when it came to her. On one side, he desperately wanted to be her hero and protect her from harm, especially if that meant stolen kisses or his heart out on his sleeve. He wanted her to fight for him, for the ranch, to be on his side. The other personality wanted to walk away from this person who was owned, physically and emotionally, by an evil mother. He couldn't seem to defend both or land on one side or the other. His reality and her reality could never live in the same sphere, not while she was being controlled by her mother.

He could always see the brutality of his father through his words or the bruises he left behind, but emotional abuse was so much more subtle and hidden. Although he could see what Brynleigh's mother was doing, he suspected it was the norm for Brynleigh. He knew she could identify the relationship with her mother as dysfunctional, however, she seemed incapable of changing the circumstances. The unhealthy pattern would continue until Brynleigh was able to stop the cycle.

Seated at the family table, Colton explained the situation to Brandon, while the ladies talked in the kitchen. "I know it's dangerous for her to be around Lucas. I mean, he probably hired someone to break in, set the fire, cut the brakes, throw the brick through the window… they're all connected, I can feel it. But she can't hide forever. Maybe the police will come up with something in the investigation, but still… What's she going to do in the meantime? And she is clearly disgusted with me. For unknown reasons. Again."

"Let Selena talk to her. She's rational, not that Brynleigh's not, but Selena's more removed from the situation. Can we pray about it?"

Colton nodded.

"Heavenly Father, this is a mess down here. Colton and Brynleigh need some direction and guidance. Brynleigh needs to know she's safe from any more harm and the police need to resolve all of these things happening and bring justice to the situation. Please intervene on their behalf. And Colton? Lord, he needs to know he's not alone. That you have his best interests, as well as Brynleigh's, at the forefront of your mind. If they are supposed to be together, help them navigate through this mess. Help us always desire to be closer to you. Amen."

Colton ran his hands over his face.

God, do you think it's a possibility you could just listen for a bit?

There were a lot of uncertainties in that prayer and God may answer them for Brandon, but not so much for him.

Colton shook hands with Brandon and nodded at Selena and Brynleigh. He'd call later to check on them, but for now, he needed to go home and reset.

Sliding into his driveway a little too hard, Colton turned off the engine. He sat for several minutes staring out the window until his brother's face popped into view.

"You going to sit there all day?" Mark rapped on the window.

"I might."

"Surly, I see." Mark stood with his hands on his hips. "You fight with Brynleigh again?"

Colton pushed out the door, moving his brother out of the way. Fight was not the term he would use.

"She didn't go for the idea of splitting up the land?"

"I didn't get the chance to tell her." Colton told him about finding the glass bee in Lucas' bathroom and the trip to the police station.

Mark whistled low. "That's some story."

"And then she got ticked at me for mentioning to the detective that I was her personal security."

"And?"

"And what? That's what I was until I quit."

"Bro, she was more than that to you. Anybody can see that."

Colton stomped up to his back door, Mark closely following. "Whose side are you on, anyway?"

"You'd do well to admit she means more to

you. Truth is an amazing thing."

"Truth? Truth is she wants to bulldoze the ranch to make money for a casino."

"That's not the truth and you know it." Mark stepped into the kitchen behind Colton even though it was clear Colton wanted to slam the door in his face. "You need to start chasing truth, Colton."

"And what's your version of the truth, Mark?"

"From my point of view, I see something alive in you I haven't seen in a long time. Something you've pushed down and buried ever since Dad got hauled away and Mom died. I see hope in your eyes when you talk about Brynleigh, and you are clearly smitten with her. And from what I've seen of Brynleigh when she came out to the ranch, she's not the type to play you. She seems honest and trustworthy. Very unlike Dad. I think you're scared and desperately want this to not work so you can keep your head, and heart, buried."

"You know you really need to shut up once in a while." Colton turned heel and left the house.

Saddling up his favorite horse and grabbing his pistol from the truck for snakes that may jump out at him, Colton walked the big bay to the edge of the barn lot and then gave it the go ahead to run like the wind. Up and down well-worn paths, over hills and through patches of woods, Colton tried to clear his head.

Chase truth, that's what his brother had said. Was truth any different than facts? Was truth more than circumstances or situations? If truth were all about the circumstances, then the truth could always change based on one's perception. That wasn't what

Mark hammered into the boys' heads. Mark said truth is truth, regardless of the circumstances. The truth about something or someone was what God said about something or someone. Not the circumstance. If that were the case, then the truth was less about the facts and more about what God said was truth. His opinion. So, what's the truth?

Colton shook his head and slowed down his horse. All of these ideas were spinning in his head and no amount of riding like the wind could blow them out.

He reached the pasture at the far back plot of their acreage and heard heavy equipment over the hill. Spurring his horse, he raced toward the sound. At the top of the crest, he brought him to a stop. Large equipment, indeed. Bulldozers pushed over small saplings and dump trucks stood ready for the next load as men scurried around shouting orders.

Colton closed his eyes and hung his head. No deadline or closure notice had been given and although they hadn't crossed property lines yet, the destruction of the ranch was imminent. He galloped down to the closest worker.

"What are you doing?" He shouted over the loud equipment.

The worker startled.

"Yo, don't run up on a guy like that." The man pulled off his ear protection and threw it on the ground.

"What are you doing?" Colton repeated himself, slower.

"What we're told to do, bro. Who are you?"

"Where's the foreman of this pony show?"

"Again, who wants to know?"

"The owner of this property." Colton got down off his horse and the gun shifted under his jacket. He was a good six inches taller than the man and forty pounds lighter, but hadn't expected to encounter anyone or anything. Colton's ears began to burn as his blood pressure started to spike. His mouth went dry. He was at his limit. If he didn't turn and walk away now, his mouth and actions would be uncontrollable. "Go get the foreman."

"Sure. Buddy, your fight's not with me. I'm just doing my job." The man turned and walked down the hill. Approaching another man in a white hard hat, Colton watched, with clenched teeth as the conversation unfolded.

Five long minutes passed, and Colton wondered what was going on. Seeing a Jeep driving fast down through all the equipment, Colton held his ground. His horse skittered sideways as the Jeep slid to a stop fifty yards away.

"Well, look who it is." Lucas jumped out of the Jeep. "I was on my way to pay you a visit when I got a call from this side of the fence saying you were here harassing the workers. Lucky me."

Colton snorted. He knew Lucas had seen the fishing wire in his pocket, knew what it was connected to. If he had been successful in getting rid of Brynleigh, getting her out of the company, the casino deal would have gone through as smooth as silk. Continually disrupting and threatening her leadership had been the play at hand. What Lucas hadn't counted on was Colton. Half owner of the property slated for the casino. Or Colton protecting

Brynleigh.

"You know you can't stop this. The paperwork has already been signed. As soon as everything has been finalized, we'll start mowing down everything on your side of the property line. How will Brynleigh feel about that? Her company mowing down her boyfriend's home?"

Boyfriend? He was no such thing. Colton took a step toward the Jeep.

"You know that I know you've been terrorizing Brynleigh."

Lucas cocked his head. "I don't think you know as much as you think you do. I bet you didn't know I was in line for the CEO position. Celeste and I had even talked about it. And then, the princess entered the picture. The long-lost daughter Celeste couldn't stand. And yet, she chose Brynleigh over me. Because I am ambitious and ruthless and Celeste knew she could control Brynleigh."

Colton hated the way Lucas said her name. Dripping with malice. "I found the glass bee in your bathroom. The one that hung in the window of Brynleigh's bookstore."

"Yes, that was a mistake." Lucas tsked.

"What was? Breaking into the store? Setting it on fire? Stealing a souvenir?" Colton drew air in through his nose. He would like nothing more than to beat the crap out of Lucas, right here, right now.

"If she would have just left on her own, Mommy Dearest would have turned it all over to me."

"Well, let's just see what the police have to say." Colton swung up on his horse. "They know, they know everything."

"If that were the case, I wouldn't be standing in front of you right now. And there's no way they can tie me to anything. Not the fire, not the brick or the brakes. None of it."

"The only way you know about brick and brakes is because you did it. And the bee is proof of the fire. Many mistakes, Lucas. A long line of mistakes, and you just admitted to them."

"Information that will never reach the authorities."

Colton pulled his horse around to face the man. Lucas' gun pointed right at him.

Chapter Twenty-One

Brynleigh sat on the wrap-around porch at Selena's, nursing a glass of tea.

She was so stupid to think there could ever be anything between her and Colton. He was stubborn, moody, unforgiving… her hero, her protector, her … Her what? Brynleigh blew out a breath. He was a mixture of good and bad, just like she was. In between all of the arguments, she'd seen a softer, kinder man she enjoyed being around. But here they were, at a standstill.

Her phone rang and she snatched it up, hoping it was Colton. Nope. It was the mechanic shop telling her that her car had been released from the police and fixed, complete with a new set of brakes. Thank goodness for insurance.

She'd never in her life been a victim and now she'd been one multiple times over. She had been a victim of her mother's manipulation for years. Everything her mother did was conditional, she recognized that now. Everything had a price.

"You okay?" Selena stepped out on the porch.

"Yeah. I was just thinking how I got in this mess." Brynleigh lifted her cell phone. "And the mechanic just called and said I could pick up my car. Can you take me?"

"Are you sure that's a good idea? What will you do after you pick up the car? Come back here?"

"I don't know. Colton seems to think Lucas is out to get me. Finding that bee kinda sealed the deal."

"I think you see the good in people and are blindsided when they don't do what you expect their good nature to do. There are evil people in this world."

"I'd think that of my mother, the evil part, if she wasn't my mother." Brynleigh stood up. "But I'm redefining that, too." After seeing her mother at the last meeting, her concern grew. She was clearly declining in her health. But then she was hateful about Colton's property and Brynleigh's role in the casino hold-up. Right back to being the same Celeste as always.

"Colton has a soft spot for you. I think you can trust that."

"Maybe. Maybe I don't trust myself."

Brynleigh followed Selena out to the car. Both were silent during the drive.

"Thank you for giving me a ride." Brynleigh leaned down to the driver's window. She could see her car, ready and waiting for her, in the lot adjacent to the office.

"Please come back out to the house. I'm still concerned about you."

"We'll see. I'll call you later." Brynleigh waved and went into the shop to pick up the keys.

In her car, Brynleigh weighed her options. She could drive back out to Selena's. And do what? Sit and wait for something to happen? For the police to change their mind and see the glass bee in Lucas' possession as relevant? For Colton to see things from her side? Or maybe not her side, but a compromise? She could go into the office. Pray she didn't run into Lucas.

Brynleigh's phone rang as she turned her vehicle towards the office.

"Hey, Juliette."

"Oh my goodness. I wasn't sure where you'd gone. Everyone disappeared. Colton left in a hurry, you were downstairs, and Lucas, smug rat that he is, vanished."

"My car was ready, so I went and picked it up," she lied. Not technically a lie. Just lots of little things left out. Like the police station visit.

Juliette nodded. "What was Colton's deal?"

"I think he likes the Bruce Willis image a little too much."

Juliette laughed. "He's just that handsome, too. Listen, I've been thinking about the bomb your mother dropped during the meeting."

"And?"

"I looked at everything and the property looks legit with all of the legal docs." Juliette hesitated. "But I want to show you something. Where are you? Maybe we could meet somewhere outside the office? Things seem a little chaotic. I'm not sure anyone else needs to know about this until you and I have talked. And the walls seem to have ears here."

"Okay. How about Reed Park over off 180th?"

"Meet you there in ten."

Brynleigh turned off the highway and exited

into an area known for its large brick houses and perfectly manicured lawns. Reed Park was a beautifully landscaped place, with its large oak trees and carefully designed flower beds. She pulled into a shady spot and waited for Juliette to arrive. What in the world was so concerning that it needed to be discussed in a private place?

Juliette pulled in next to her and jumped into the passenger side of Brynleigh's car.

"What is so important?" Brynleigh fanned through the stack of papers Juliette handed her. "These aren't the casino papers. These are my employment papers."

"I know. Look at the pages I marked and the highlighted areas."

Brynleigh flipped to the yellow mark. Irrevocable Trust. "This is what I signed. I don't get it."

"It's an irrevocable trust which means nothing can be changed without a court order. Celeste can't just come in and change parts of your contract because she wants to. It's written in black and white that you have full control over every project and every detail of every project. She can't pick and choose. It's all or nothing. She signed these. You can't tell me she didn't know what she was signing. All her lawyers looked over the documents."

"But why would she create an irrevocable trust if the plan was for me to only be in an acting capacity until she was well enough to take back the reins?"

"Maybe she didn't think she would get better."

"That's crazy. Mother is invincible. Nothing can take her down."

"Maybe she thought this cancer would."

"That's a little morbid. Why did she say what she did in the meeting if she knew she couldn't do that?"

"Your mother is not above a little intimidation. I think it was a scare tactic, and she wasn't counting on you bucking the system or letting a relationship get in the way of business."

Not sure there is a relationship there, but Juliette didn't know all that had happened in the last twenty-four hours.

"This all seems a little far-fetched to me. Mother is brilliant and wouldn't get beat at her own game."

"Looks like she tripped herself up this time."

"Does this mean I can stop the casino deal?"

"I think so, but why? You have the opportunity to make a smart business move here. Turn the direction of the property, keep the ranch intact, have your cake and eat it, too."

"Sounds like my mother isn't the only head full of brains."

"Go tell Colton, and then meet me at the office. We'll fly this under the radar for the moment until we can get the contractors and architects together to change the casino plans."

"What about Lucas?"

"He doesn't need to know yet. But, I'll warn you, he's going to be furious. If you thought you had a target on your back before…"

"You're amazing, Juliette."

"Yes, yes I am. I deserve a raise, you know." Juliette said as she got back in her car.

She did, indeed. And that target on her back? It had just grown exponentially.

~

Colton slid his hand into his jacket. The pistol he carried for snakes sat heavy on his waistband. He kept his eyes trained on Lucas', ready for any move. If he was going to have to draw, it had to be fast. Lucas' gun was already up. No telling how good a shot he was.

"What are you going to do, shoot me?" Colton hollered. "You've got all these witnesses."

"If they know what's good for them, they'll stay quiet or be out of a job." Lucas stepped out of the Jeep.

Lucas advanced toward him in slow motion, drawing out every step. Colton's blood pounded in his ears and his mouth was dry. Colton blinked rapidly. A vision of Bandit lying still flashed before him. His men and he were trapped. The sound of far-off gunfire echoed in his ears. The enemy was closer, closer than Colton had expected. Colton felt pain radiate through his leg. His head began to throb, and he started the inhale/exhale motion to stop the fog from crowding in. This was not then. He was in Texas, not Afghanistan. Colton shook the flashback away.

Lucas took two more steps toward him and Colton stiffened. One more move. Breathe in… 1…2…3…4, and out. Lucas was almost on top of him.

"Do not come in closer." Colton growled. The darkness was creeping in.

"Or what?" Lucas sidestepped.

Colton pulled his gun as Lucas stepped around a cactus. The fog in his brain turned red as he squeezed the trigger. Lucas cried out, blood oozing through his shirt.

Sliding down his horse, Colton dropped the gun and crumpled to the ground. He pounded his fist into the dirt and then succumbed to the flashback. The volley of gunfire squeezed out all other sounds. Get Bandit. Stay down. You've been hit. We're coming for you. His men pulling him to safety. Bandit's blood intertwined with his own.

Colton opened his left eye, the right one caked with dirt. The shooting had stopped. A black boot kicked his gun farther away. He attempted to pull into a crouched position, but his legs refused to cooperate.

"Colton Bruens? Just stay where you are. Officer Jeffers is going to cuff you for your protection and mine. Just lay still."

Colton squinted up into the sun. Blistering fire ran up his spine. The officer gently pulled his arms to his back, turning his face into the dirt.

"Easy now, son. Just be easy." The officer above him squatted next to him. "Colton, can you hear me? Nod your head if you can."

Colton nodded.

"Sir, should I sit him up?"

"Just give him a minute."

Colton blinked and then rolled to his side and up on his buttocks. Startled, the younger officer jumped to his feet.

"You good, son? Know where you are?"

Colton pursued his lips and blew out a breath.

The fog was beginning to subside. He resisted the urge to curse and spit into the dust instead. "Mark."

"I'm here." Mark put his hand on Colton's shoulder. Beyond him, Colton could see an ambulance, lights flashing, no siren. "Captain. I heard the shot and got here as fast as I could. I had a bad feeling."

"Well, it's not good." The captain looked at the ambulance loading Lucas. "One of the construction guys thought there might be an altercation, and they were right. I guess your brother shot the other guy, wounded him superficially."

"Do you know who the other guy was?"

"Don't know yet. I'm sure we'll find out, though." The captain hesitated. "You've probably witnessed this, since you live with him, but when we arrived, I'm pretty sure your brother was in the midst of a PTS flareup. I've seen it before, even experienced it before, but you probably already know how serious those can become if left untreated."

Mark reached out and shook the captain's hand. "I did not know about the PTSD."

Colton started shaking his head.

The captain grimaced. "We don't call it PTSD. He doesn't have a disorder, not yet anyways. He has triggers that bring on responses post-trauma. A disorder implies he's broken and he's not. But he could be if he doesn't deal with it. Understand, son?" The captain bent over and looked in Colton's eyes.

"Yes, sir." Colton nodded.

"We'll be taking him to county. You can arrange bail there."

"And the other guy?" Mark hooked his neck at

the retreating ambulance.

"We'll take him to the hospital first, and then figure this out from there."

Chapter Twenty-Two

Brynleigh drove to the ranch, her heartbeat moving at a faster speed than her speedometer. She'd make Colton hear her out and he'd realize she was on his side. She could save the ranch, just like he'd saved her so many times.

When she arrived, Colton's truck was by his house, but no one answered the door. She drove up the lane to the main farmhouse and knocked on its screen door. A woman she'd met briefly when she'd first visited the ranch many moons ago, answered.

"Yes?"

"I'm looking for Colton. Or Mark. Are either of them home?"

"And you are?"

"Brynleigh Tavish."

"Oh, Brynleigh. You've got both my boys in quite a stir." The woman came out of the house and gestured for Brynleigh to sit. A slight breeze blew around the corner of the house and riffled the woman's bangs.

Brynleigh tried to remember what Colton had said about his mother. Squinting her eyes, she could not come up with one conversation where Colton mentioned his mother or his father, in fact.

"Are you Colton's mother?" she asked hesitantly.

"Oh goodness, no. But I guess I inferred that, didn't I? I'm their aunt, their mother's sister, Eunice."

"Nice to meet you. I think we met briefly when I was out here last." They were good people doing good things, and she had first-hand knowledge from her tour of the ranch with Mark. "What do you mean by 'stirring up your boys'?"

"Mark was confident you'd find a way to save the ranch. Colton, not so much. But then it looked like he was at war with himself over you every time your name was mentioned. His face would cloud up, and then he'd break into a smile. I think he may have crazy feelings for you."

Brynleigh blushed. Crazy feelings? That was mutual. Her heart pounded.

"Are either of them here? I have good news for them." She really wanted to tell Colton first, but Mark would be anxious to hear it as well.

"Here's Mark now." Eunice gestured at the 4-wheeler pulling up to the porch.

Both women stood.

"Brynleigh. I didn't expect you to be here."

"I know. I've got some news-"

"Can it wait for half a second? I've got to call Brandon." Mark climbed the steps and sat on the top stoop.

"Sure."

"Hey, Brandon. Mark here. Listen, Colton's in jail…yes, I know… The sheriff said they'd probably release him… he had a… yes… I can't leave…. Thanks, friend." Mark hung up the phone and turned to Brynleigh and his aunt.

"Colton's where?" Brynleigh heard her voice raise several octaves.

"Heading to jail. He shot some guy on the construction site over where they're building that casino."

Brynleigh's head started to spin. Colton was heading to jail? Because he'd shot someone? By the casino site that wasn't legally given a green light yet? Her brain turned topsy-turvy as she attempted to process what Mark said. "Wait. What?"

"And why can't you go bail him out?" His aunt chided him. She didn't look nearly as undone by all the information as Brynleigh did.

"The sheriff told me to wait here. He'd send someone over to get my statement." Mark shrugged. "That's why I called Brandon."

"The construction wasn't supposed to start yet. I haven't signed off on anything."

"It hasn't, not on our property at least. But it has, across from ours. I don't know how all that works, but the guy Colton shot seemed to be the one pushing it through. I guess the other guy pulled a gun on Colton first."

The one pushing it through. Lucas? Why was he at the construction site?

"Did you get a look at the guy?"

"No, they already had him on the gurney and ready to load up."

"Oh no. I hope that wasn't-" No need to draw Mark and his aunt into the politics of Texas A&D.

"Brandon will take care of Colton. I forgot to ask, why are you here, Brynleigh?"

"Kinda a long story and I'll spare you the details, but I found a way to save the ranch."

"So did we. But Colton didn't get a chance to tell you."

"He was a little upset with me when we spoke last." Brynleigh hung her head.

Eunice wrung her hands.

"Huh. Well, we talked about selling a portion of the property off to the east to the casino people, but leaving the homestead and farmhouse and outlying barns in our name. It's a win-win situation."

"That's an idea." Should she divulge her news?

"Brynleigh, you said you had something you wanted to share," Eunice piped up.

"I think it had better wait now, until I can share it with Colton first."

"Do you want to wait here?"

"No, I'll go on home. Would you call me when he does get home? I can come back over. It really should be face-to-face because of our last conversation."

"Can do. Aunt Eunice, I'm going to start writing my statement." Eunice followed Mark into the house.

~

"Tell me the story one more time." The sheriff nodded at him.

Colton laid his head down on the hardwood, no-nonsense table he was handcuffed to. "It's not a story. These are facts."

"Just lay it out for me again."

"I was out riding, heard the heavy equipment, went to check it out, got in an argument with one of the workers, and he called the foreman. Lucas, the guy I shot, showed up saying he was coming for me anyway, and this was great timing. He drew his gun first, and I shot him. I was defending myself." Colton ticked off the facts on his fingers. "Did you find his gun?"

"We did. What do you mean 'coming for you'?"

"He's behind all of the crimes towards Brynleigh. The fire, the brick, the cut brakes."

"And Brynleigh is? How do you know that?"

Colton groaned. This was going nowhere fast. "You have all the reports here or at the police department. Brynleigh is Brynleigh Tavish, my boss, sort of."

"Man, you are talking in riddles. Brynleigh Tavish is your boss?"

"Yes. I'm her personal security. Or I was." That added a new rabbit hole to the many he'd already created.

"And this Lucas character?"

"He works for Brynleigh, too."

"So, this was a lover's quarrel."

Colton put his head back down on the table. He would never be able to unravel these knots. "No."

"Captain, we have someone out here that wants to talk to you about this case." An officer ducked into the room.

"Okay, let's take a break. If you have to draw pictures in order for me to connect all the dots to this case, that's what we're doing next."

Colton sighed. If he hadn't shot Lucas, the man would have shot him. And at that close range? He would have been dead in his tracks. Lucas said he was on his way to find him and Colton had walked right into his plans. He knew what Lucas was capable of. The man had admitted everything to Colton. In order to gain the highly prized seat at Texas A&D, Brynleigh needed to be scared off. All of the things from the beginning 911 call had been to get Brynleigh off the throne she never wanted in the first place.

"Well, today is your lucky day, son." The captain re-entered the interview room. "Your neighbor, Brandon, just happens to be friends with several of my deputies. They dug up the reports you mentioned, and everything does point to this Lucas guy. We're going to release you into Brandon's recognizance with the understanding that you will have to go to court for the assault charge."

"Assault charge?" Colton stood up, cuffs still chained to the table.

"You shot someone. You have to give account for that. Even if it was self-defense, you still need to tell the judge what happened." The captain unhooked his handcuffs. "And, son? You need to talk to someone. We both know what happened out there."

Colton looked at the floor. He knew he did. Just verbalizing 'talk to someone' made him cringe. He'd think about it. Maybe Brandon knew of someone who would be a safe start.

Brandon stood when Colton entered the waiting room.

"All of the papers are signed, son. You're free

to go."

Colton shook the captain's hand. "Thank you, sir."

"You can thank me by doing what we talked about in there." The Captain hooked his thumb at the hallway leading to the interview room.

"Yes, sir."

Brandon led the way to his truck, Colton following behind him. Silently, they drove out of town. "Mind if I ask a question?"

"No." Colton cast a sideways glance at Brandon.

"What was the Captain talking about?"

"He thinks I have PTS."

"Do you?"

"Probably. I just thought I had it handled."

Brandon nodded his head. "From the military?"

Colton looked out the window at the scenery flying by. If he were truthful with Brandon, the military hadn't been his first traumatic episode. He was pretty sure he could trust Brandon. They'd continued to cross paths all through the Brynleigh drama, and Brandon had proven he had his back on all occasions.

"It started before that. My dad beat on my mom when I was a kid. Rage has been my go-to emotion since then."

"That's a tough one."

"I started drinking in high school, just to dull the anger. Sometimes it worked, sometimes it just made it worse. When I enlisted, I had no idea how good it would feel to unleash that anger."

Brandon stayed silent.

"The Captain thinks I disappeared into a black hole when Lucas threatened to shoot me. He believes Lucas is responsible for everything else, but he doesn't want me to end up trapped in the past, reliving it. I suppose I do need to talk some of that out."

"Sounds like it catches up with you now and again."

"My lieutenant was constantly in my face about being reckless. I didn't really care. My squad got things done and up until the last mission, I brought everyone home safely. Just that last mission-" Colton put a hand over his eyes. The moisture surprised him, but he decided he didn't care. Brandon could think what he wanted. He was broken. A broken man not able to control himself, anger rotting his insides. All he wanted at that moment was a drink, which wouldn't cover him long enough to get free of the pain. That's what it really was. Pain. He'd stood by and gotten angry at his father for laying his hands on his mother. He was angry at his mother for surviving his dad's fists, but not cancer. He was angry at his brother and his ability to turn it all over to God. Where was God in all of this? Maybe God only cared about Mark. And Brandon. Not Colton. He was defective. Unworthy.

Colton gripped the sides of his head.

"Okay, okay. We're stopping up here. We need to talk." Brandon pulled over.

"No, please. Not here." Colton started to rock.

Brandon looked around. A cemetery sat on the right and an open pasture on the left. "Is this where your mom is buried?"

Colton nodded.

"We can go somewhere else." Brandon started to pull away.

"No, it's fine." How convenient. He missed his mom, despite the anger. "She's down around the corner. Second row on the left."

"Do you want to go down to her gravesite?" At Colton's nod, he drove into the cemetery, down the grass-grown lane and parked just past a small bench. A very large oak tree shaded the first two rows of headstones.

The cemetery was beautiful with its old trees and decorated gravesites.

Colton climbed out of the truck, slouching. He walked over to the headstone with his mom's name etched in the granite. He and his brother hadn't had much, but they'd managed to scrape enough together for a nice marker.

He bent down and traced her name.

"This is a pretty big plot. Is it for other family members as well?"

Colton felt Brandon watching him.

"One for me and one for my brother, on either side of Mom." Colton pointed.

"Oh."

Colton sat down on the side he'd pointed to as his. He pulled his knees up to his chest and tried to control his breathing. In…1 …2… 3… 4. Out… 1… 2… 3. The sobs came unexpectedly. He sensed Brandon move over to the iron bench, close enough to help, but far enough away to let Colton do what he needed to do. Tears drenched his shirt.

Stretching out on the dirt that would someday

hold his own body, Colton laid his head on his arms and cried. Cried like he'd never cried at his mom's funeral or for his buddies killed in action. The first he had no control over except he hadn't protected her from a ruthless, evil man. He'd been just a boy. The second had been his fault. He'd just been following orders when they swept through the village searching for Afghan insurgents, however, he was reckless with devastating results. He hadn't been strong enough to stand up to his father, nor did he fully protect the men serving under him. He wasn't brave enough, capable enough, or worthy of any respect. He should have taken the punches instead of allowing his mother to get beat up. He should have died instead of his men. Colton let his tears mingle with the dirt, the hollowness and anger leaking out of his soul like battery acid.

A soft breeze brought memories of his mother's voice whispering her favorite Bible verses in the night. Even when the cancer had spread and she was wracked in pain, his mom had always turned to her God.

Even though I walk through the valley of the shadow of death, I will fear no evil for you are with me.

Be strong and courageous…

Do not fear…

The soft, sweet voice of his mother changed to a solid, peaceful yet strong voice that Colton had never heard before.

Come dwell in the shelter of the Most High. Come abide in the shadow of the Almighty. I will be your refuge and your fortress. I will cover you with my wings and give you refuge. I will be with you in times of trouble. I will rescue you.

God?

Let me be your Savior and your shield. Cast all your cares on me. I know the plans I have for you. Let me restore you and fill you with grace and peace.

Oh God. I need you. I've never really believed in you, but Mom did. And Mark does. I've been so angry for so long. I'm not sure I know how to release that. Not in a good way. I've failed so many people. I'm not worthy like Brandon or Mark. I'm not sure what you want from me. Show me like you do Mark. I hear all of these verses in my head and can't possibly believe they are for me. But if they are, if you want me, please help me understand. I'm like that Tin Man at Brynleigh's, empty inside. Or maybe not so empty. Not filled with good things, for sure. I don't know what I'm doing or what I'm supposed to be doing. I need you.

Colton could feel the wind brush past him, hear the birds chirping in the trees. The weight on his chest eased, and his head stopped its tilt-a-whirl swinging. A calm and peaceful feeling came over him in gentle waves and he continued to weep.

Please keep me in your presence forever.

Colton stood up and walked over to the bench where Brandon waited. The men embraced, with tears flowing down their faces.

"Bro–" Colton started.

"I know. You had a moment over there, didn't you? I can see it all over you. That and the snot coming from your nose."

Colton laughed and wiped his nose on his shirt.

"I want to do that again. Every day."

Brandon punched his shoulder. "What? Lay in the dirt?"

"Ha ha. No, listen to God's voice."

"That is pretty cool, isn't it? Not everyone can hear it as audibly as you clearly did, but you can talk to Him every single minute of the day."

Colton nodded. "I plan on it. I'm ready to go home now. You?"

"Yep. Are you going to talk to Brynleigh any time soon?"

"I'll go get my truck and head over there now."

"Sounds like a plan."

Chapter Twenty-Three

Brynleigh sat by the phone, wishing it would ring. Of course, no such luck. At least not while she was watching it. Grabbing a Coke from the fridge, she laid back down on the couch and tried to watch stupid comedies. Anything to keep her eyes off the phone. Mark said he'd call, but that had been hours ago. Maybe she should call him, check in and make sure he hadn't forgotten her.

"Mark, this is Brynleigh. Have you heard from Colton or Brandon yet?" She sounded like a mothering hen or a controlling girlfriend. It wasn't controlling to want to know where Colton was at, was it? Maybe he didn't want her to know where he was. Maybe he was still angry with her.

"I don't know anything yet, Brynleigh. Let me check in with Brandon and I'll call you back. I'm worried, too."

"Thank you. And Mark? If he doesn't want to talk to me, I understand. I want to make sure he's okay, but I know he may be still–"

"Brynleigh, that brother of mine may be bull headed and foolish at times, but he's not stupid, and he's clearly very smitten with you. He'll come around. I'll call you back in a bit."

Brynleigh breathed out a sigh she'd been holding. She hoped Colton's brother was right. Flipping through channels, she tried to busy herself with one eye on her phone. Countless times of checking it to make sure the ringer was turned up and not muted.

She put the last load of laundry in when she heard her phone go off.

Mark. Not Colton.

"Hey Brynleigh. I just talked to Brandon, and he said he dropped him off at home and that Colton was planning to come see you. I can't see the house from here so I don't know if he's left yet. Sometime soon, though, I suspect."

"Okay, thanks." She'd better tidy up. She still hadn't had the opportunity to tell him her news yet. Maybe he wouldn't want to hear it. Maybe he was coming over to tell her that whatever this was between them was over. Brynleigh shook her head. Maybe she should tell herself to shut up and listen.

Several hours passed and no Colton. He should have been here by now. What if he'd changed his mind and wasn't interested in talking to her? No, he was going to talk to her or at least listen. This merry-go-around was stopping now.

Brynleigh scrawled out a note that she'd return home soon and taped it to the front door, just in case he did show up. Pulling her car out of the garage, she headed to Colton's ranch.

Regardless of how Colton perceived her now, she needed to see him. Needed to tell him how she could save the ranch. Who was she kidding? She wanted to see him, to tell him the ranch could be saved, but more importantly, that she may be falling in love with him. Whoa, girl. The L-word? She only knew love from her mother. And she and Colton hadn't even dated. This was something very different. A shared feeling, she was certain. This wasn't a you do this for me and I'll do that for you. They genuinely cared for each other. Were they willing to risk it all to prove it? Look how many times he'd stepped in and saved her? He was more than her hero, he was the person she wanted to share life with. She would choose love over fear with Colton. He was not like her mother. He wasn't. Hopefully, they'd separate their feelings for each other from the saving of the ranch. Happy as she was that she could save the ranch for him, she was more hopeful he saw beyond her actions to her feelings and didn't think the two were connected. That would be something her mother would do. Save something special with the expectation of getting something in return.

Brynleigh slowed down as the road narrowed. The streetlights were few and far between this far out of the city.

Light bounced off a truck grill to the left in a ditch.

Was that–?

Brynleigh braked hard and jumped out of her car. Running back to the spot where she'd seen the truck, she passed by a bloody, very dead deer. Using her phone flashlight, Brynleigh slipped down the hill until she could reach the driver's door.

"Colton!" She knocked on the window at the

unresponsive body in the driver's seat. She pulled on the door handle, but it only creaked part way open and stopped with a screech. Brynleigh reached in sideways and touched his arm.

With a groan, Colton picked his head up from the steering wheel. The whole left side of his face was oozing blood. Brynleigh tried not to react when he swung his head toward her.

"Brynleigh?"

"Shh… it's me. I'm calling an ambulance. Stay still until they can assess the damages." Brynleigh dialed 911 and told them where they were.

"Don't leave me."

Brynleigh leaned in to hear what he was saying. She took hold of his hand and squeezed his fingers. "I'm not going anywhere."

"Good. Now you're my superhero."

No. No, she was not. She was nobody's hero, least of all, his.

"Now I owe you."

Oh my. He needed to stop talking. He owed her nothing. That was her mother's language. Maybe they weren't on the same page.

Within a short time, a firetruck and ambulance pulled alongside the curb and worked their way down to the truck. A flurry of movement and Colton was out of the truck and strapped to a gurney.

"Do you want to ride in the ambulance with him?" An EMT asked.

"Uh no, I'll follow you if that's okay." She wasn't family. She didn't even know if they were still friends. He'd wanted her to stay with him, but did that mean in the ambulance as well? She'd call Mark on the way and fill him in. Then she'd sit in the waiting room and wait.

~

Colton opened his eyes to the soft light in the corner of the room. A figure slumped in the chair next to the hospital bed.

He cleared his throat. "Hey."

Brynleigh scrambled to his side. "Hi. How are you feeling?"

Colton lifted the tubes running from his hand to the IV above his head.

"You were in an accident. You passed out after they got you in the ambulance. They're going to run tests to make sure you don't have a concussion. Mark said to call him when you woke up."

"Just wait a minute." Colton touched the bandage wrapped around his head.

"You had a nasty gash on your forehead." Brynleigh pulled his hands down with her own.

Colton locked eyes with her and held onto her hands.

"Brynleigh, I don't know if you know what all has happened since we last talked." Colton rubbed his thumb on the palm of her hand. "I was on my way to you."

"I know some of it. You shot Lucas, he went to the hospital. You went to jail. I found out some things at work so I went to find you. Lucky I did, because you were in the ditch."

"Wow, those are a whole lot of pieces to put together, but not all of them. With those things you know, I'm surprised you're here now." Colton couldn't take his eyes off her. She was disheveled from sleeping in the chair and according to the mascara on her cheeks, she'd been crying at some point. She was more beautiful than anything he'd ever seen. "But, I'm glad you are."

"Colton, I don't know how you feel about–"

"Us?"

"I was going to say me. I've been rude and uncompromising and ungrateful…" Brynleigh pulled her hands from his.

"Brynleigh, I've been smitten with you since day one." He smiled at her smile. "What's so funny?"

"I have never heard a guy say 'smitten' in my life."

"It's the way I feel."

"Like me becoming a puddle at your feet when you're around?" She grinned wider.

"Or a firecracker. We tend to set off bombs and then leap out of the way." Colton scratched his chin, noting the scruffy growth. "Now that we got all the sappy stuff out of the way…"

"Are we done?" Brynleigh pouted. She leaned over the bed, her hair brushing his arm, eyes intent on his.

"No. Come here." Colton tried to adjust his body so she could be closer to him, but the bed alarm went off.

Brynleigh laughed and sat back in her chair as a nurse came in, chiding Colton on not getting out of bed without help. The nurse tapped his fall-risk bracelet and warned him.

"Guess that can wait." Brynleigh winked at him. "Tell me your story and then I'll tell you mine."

Colton's gaze lingered on hers.

"Okay." He adjusted the sheets on the narrow bed. "I was so agitated when we got done at the police station…" He reached for her hand. Without hesitation, she scooted her chair as close as possible and put her cold fingers in his. "I went out riding and heard the heavy machinery so close to my property. I was fuming by the time I reached the top of the hill. They'd already started digging for the casino, not on my property yet, but so close. The poor guy I talked to first didn't seem to have a clue what I was talking about so he went and got the foreman."

"Lucas?"

"No, he was just a foreman on the project. Apparently, I was creating enough of a stir that they called the sheriff."

"Wow. What about Lucas?"

"He was on his way to the ranch to confront me about the bee. He'd seen it in my pocket, or the fishing wire attached to it." Colton hesitated and smiled at her. "Sorry, you make me forget my words."

"Same."

"Anyway, Lucas confessed to everything. From breaking into your store to scare you, the brick, cutting the brakes, everything. He knew your mother was bringing you in even before you did."

"Why? Why would he do that?" Brynleigh sat up straighter in her chair.

"He wanted your position, the one your mother brought you in for. He thought he could scare you out of it. You already knew it was a cutthroat business, his scare tactics confirmed it."

"Those are some pretty hefty scare tactics, but

lines up with Juliette's thoughts, too. Someone could have gotten badly hurt."

"Yeah, you. Greed got in the way with him, I guess."

"Did the sheriff hear all of these confessions?"

"No, unfortunately. All the sheriff saw was me shooting back at him and then flipping out." Colton grimaced. He'd hoped to keep his trauma reaction out of the conversation until he could talk to someone, but apparently it was no longer supposed to be hidden. He remembered those whisperings in the cemetery, he needed to lean into God and let Him do His thing.

"Colton, what does that mean 'flipping out'?"

Great. Twice in one day, he had to explain his actions.

"Because of trauma in my past, I occasionally resort back to those times and respond like I would have then, but not how I appropriately should now." He'd spare her the details and cause.

"Are you talking PTSD?"

Colton cringed. "Yes, but I don't have a disorder. Just stress from traumatic events in my past." Please don't ask from what. He wasn't ready to downplay his father, he really wanted to hold on to that anger for a bit. Based on his conversation with God, though, that may be the one thing holding him back from freedom. The anger and bitterness, maybe it was time to let go.

Thankfully, Brynleigh didn't ask any more questions. "Is Lucas at this hospital?"

~

"Your bullet only grazed him. He was released

from the hospital before you came in. Brandon said they took him straight from here to the jail. My guess is everything lined up with the police reports. Hopefully, he'll confess to the sheriff." Brynleigh rubbed her fingers over his palm.

"Okay, then. It was self-defense, but I didn't aim to kill him."

"I think they knew that." Brynleigh wadded up her hair and stuck a pencil in it to hold it on top of her head. "Let me tell you my side now."

"First, can you help me turn so I can see you better without craning my neck? And without causing the bed alarm to go off?" Colton reached for her and slid his hand without the IV over her shoulder. She leaned into him as he moved his knees over to the side. He was dangerously close to her face, and he brushed his lips on hers. She leaned farther onto the bed, but pulled away abruptly when the bed alarm went off for a second time.

"For Pete's sake," Colton mumbled. Brynleigh giggled.

"I'm not exactly sure why your alarm keeps going off…" the same nurse from before bustled into the room.

"I'm not trying to get out of bed. Does it go off when extra weight is added to the bed?"

"Extra weight?" The nurse looked at Colton and then Brynleigh. "Oh… let me adjust that setting."

Colton and Brynleigh laughed at the nurse's reaction.

"Anyway, I was heading to the office after picking up my car…" Brynleigh backpedaled at the look on his face. "I know, I know. I thought I was safe. Lucas didn't know I was with you or that we had gone to the police station. On my way there, Juliette called and asked to meet me offsite. Celeste and I signed an irrevocable trust document when I first started. The lawyers looked it over and advised her to set it up that way, but I don't know why she would've done that. Juliette thinks she was sicker than she let on. At a meeting, she took me off the casino project, because I wasn't moving fast enough, and Lucas led her to believe that the reason I was dragging my heels was you. She knew she couldn't back out of the trust legally, but she was pretty convincing. She can't do that. She was just trying to scare me. My contract stated everything was now under my control, and my signature had to be on everything. Mother couldn't take back projects on a whim. It was either she take back the whole corporation through a court order or let me lead. No picking parts. So, I saved the ranch. We win."

Colton pursed his lips.

"Didn't we?" Brynleigh chewed on a cuticle.

"I'm so tired of keeping score. I don't want to win. I want to be happy. Everything is so conditional and a prize to be won. I don't want that anymore."

"I saved your ranch. You can keep the ranch."

"Mark and I had a proposition for you, but the more I got to know you, I realized things don't matter as much as relationships do. More importantly, our relationship. Brynleigh, God is really showing me things right now, and the best one is, while I would hate to lose the ranch, losing you would be worse. You saved me." Colton brushed his thumb across her lips.

"Despite our arguments, you saved me. I never wanted a relationship like my mother and father's. I want one like Brandon and Selena's. You showed me glimpses of what could be. I want you in my life. You kept saying how I saved you, and it just reinforced that I can't save you. I'm not even doing a good job protecting you or the ranch. I care about you and not to get all mushy-gushy, but it goes beyond feelings. I have to take action. And if I can't take that action then I have to rely on someone else."

"You're pushing me off on someone else?"

"Yeah, God."

"Oh."

"This has nothing to do with the ranch or what you can or cannot do. What I feel isn't conditional on what you do. I have to trust Him to take care of you when I can't."

"Oh."

"I'm not going to be good at this. It looks like trust is an issue for both of us. And quite frankly, I don't trust emotions, but I believe God opened this door for us, and we'd be fools not to try."

"That's the second time I've heard about God and these doors. Colton, I'll be honest with you," Brynleigh hesitated. "I'm struggling with the God stuff. I see Selena and Brandon believing in God, and how happy they are. And then you've started talking about God, and quite frankly, I don't know who that is or why he'd want anything to do with me. What does He want? Is He like my mother?"

"I know it's hard to believe especially since you can't see Him. But, no, He isn't like your mother.

Far from it. My mother believed He created us and loves us. She turned to Him at every step in her life and trusted Him fully. Like Selena and Brandon do."

"Didn't your mother die? And was a victim of domestic abuse? Why did she trust God?"

"Brynleigh, I'm trying to figure all of this out myself, and I grew up hearing about God all the time. These are some pretty weighted questions. I'm really tired, too. Can we circle back around on these questions later?"

"Of course." Brynleigh scrambled up into his hospital bed, careful not to bump his IV hand.

"Don't set the bed alarm off." Colton adjusted so she was in the crux of his chest.

"The nurse fixed it, remember?"

"Wonderful." When Bryleigh turned her face up to his, Colton soundly kissed her. There would be time for more talk later, but for now, the here and now was all that mattered.

Epilogue

6 months later

"Juliette, it's so good to see you." Brynleigh wrapped her arms around her friend, catching the large salad bowl between them. "Your trip to Italy suited you nicely. You're all tan and relaxed."

"Two weeks in my favorite place? You bet." Juliette laughed. "Where do you want this?"

"Hmmm… is it your special 7-layer salad?" Brynleigh tucked the bowl into the refrigerator. "And the Mexican wedding cookies?"

"Of course. Special ordered." Juliette pulled a plastic container out of her carrying bag.

"My goodness, I love these things." Brynleigh stuck a small one in her mouth and then brushed the obligatory powdered sugar off her shirt.

"Looks like you've got a table full of people coming."

"Family, the boys," Bryleigh busied herself with adjusting the items on the counter. "Brandon and Selena."

"I'm sorry I wasn't around after your mother's funeral. I could have helped more." Juliette sighed.

"How are you feeling?"

"It's ok. You had that trip planned for a long time. Besides, there were a lot of meetings with lawyers and contract paperwork to go through. Things I had to do."

"Yeah, well, I'm still sorry. Two-edged sword, I guess, with Lucas not being there either. You didn't have him to update you on properties or try to kill you."

"Very funny. Supposedly, he has a court date in the fall that I'll attend. And then the trial afterwards. The lawyers may call you as a witness even though you didn't have actual knowledge of anything. Character witness, maybe."

"I expected that."

"As far as how I am? I'm ok. It's weird knowing Mother's not out there, trying to manipulate me into doing her bidding or conspiring against the next poor soul. I keep forgetting she's gone. I guess that's normal."

"I think so. My mom's been gone for a long time. She wasn't the presence your mother was, but I still think, 'I should call Mom and tell her…' and then remember she's gone."

"Do you think she ever loved me?" Brynleigh's eyes filled up.

"Brynleigh–"

"Hey, Juliette." Colton paused in the doorway, looking at one woman and then the other. "What happened?" He went over to Brynleigh and put his arms around her. "Brynleigh?"

"We were just talking about my mother." Her voice muffled against his crisp shirt. He smelled good, fresh from a shower. If she wasn't careful, she'd leave mascara tracks down his shirt. She pulled away from him. "I don't know if I'll ever really know. I wanted to please her, knowing I never could. You saw the way she was. Not only cutthroat with the corporation, but also me. Confident in me while we were in front of others, but then harsh and unforgiving when no one was around. It took a lot of convincing and deep soul searching, but Colton, and God, showed me that's not real love."

Juliette nodded her head. "I always wondered how she could be two very different people."

Colton pulled her in close again. "Remember what we talked about? It wasn't her actions that defined you. Not then and not now. Only God can do that. You are only responsible for you and your actions. What you know is God loves you even more than I do, if I were so inclined to say those words…"

Brynleigh swatted at him. He was right. She'd need to forgive her mother and put it behind her. Even at the funeral, where they'd had to rent out a large church to hold all the people, Brandon and Selena's pastor had talked about forgiveness.

"You know the truth, Juliette. Keep reminding her." Colton said to Juliette as he walked out of the kitchen.

"Wait, Colton. How are you so wise?" Juliette asked.

"I've been chasing my own demons for so long, and I'm finally free." Colton paused. "Only by God's grace, though."

"Yes, by the grace of God." Juliette echoed.

~

Colton walked out onto the porch and watched Brandon's silver truck pull into the ranch's drive. He took a deep breath and listened to the sounds around him. Life, and God, had been good to him. Brynleigh and he had been studying the Bible with Brandon and Selena, and it was soul-deep stuff. They both had a lot of baggage and he'd realized that although he'd been given a rough hand with his father's abuse, he was not his father. He did not have to respond in the way his father responded. He was not his father, he repeated to himself often, praying one day he'd fully believe it. The anger that welled up inside him, threatening to spill out with his fists, did not have the same power it used to have.

Brandon consistently held him accountable for things Colton could control. He was forever asking, "Is that truth?" when Colton spouted off something negative. Colton didn't feel the need to defend his position or to justify it. He had enough respect for Brandon to honestly seek the truth. And God… Well, He'd shown up in a big way. Not only had He shown Colton he was valuable and worthy of respect and love, but He'd also shown Colton how to encourage Brynleigh. How to convince her God was more than some being up in the sky. How to show her love and not the kind she'd experienced from her mother. He was finding he did love Brynleigh, scary though it may be.

Brynleigh was blossoming in her relationship with God, just as Colton was. Baby steps. That's what the pastor told them when they both fully surrendered their lives during an altar call. Neither of them knew exactly what that looked like, but the pastor encouraged them to learn all they could about who God was through daily prayer and studying the Bible.

After her mother's death and Lucas' arrest, he watched her step confidently into the President position at Texas A&D. A portion of Colton and Mark's property would be sold to the corporation for the casino, leaving the homestead intact, and the casino's front entrance turned to the north, so the heaviest of traffic would not go past the ranch. Win-win outcome.

On top of all that, Colton loved watching Brynleigh connect with the boys on the ranch, teaching them computer skills and English or Algebra in the evenings. Her face would light up when one of the boys attempted something hard. In her eyes, they were always successful, regardless of the outcome, but always because they tried. She was in her element, just like at the bookstore. Quite frankly, anywhere. She was that kind of person. One he always wanted to be around.

And plans for the new bookstore were designed and ready to be executed. Another Texas A&D project, but one that had Brynleigh's flair and not her mother's.

Colton shook his head and stepped off the porch. He'd been thinking so hard about Brynleigh that he'd failed to see his friends get out of the truck and step in front of him.

"Wow, wandering a bit?" Brandon shook his hand.

Colton hem-hawed.

"Apparently, Brynleigh is already here, based

on your love-sick look." Selena hugged him. "I saw that same look on Brandon's face often enough. With me, of course."

"I heard no complaints from you." Brandon kissed his wife.

Colton laughed. "They're all in the kitchen."

"Everyone's here now. I'll have Aunt Eunice call the boys in." Mark opened the screen door for them.

Brandon acknowledged Mark with a handshake and let Selena enter the house. Pausing at the door, he called over his shoulder, "Hey, Colton, we left the guard down on the gate so everyone could come through okay, but someone pulled in after us."

Mark stepped back out of the house.

"Do you know the vehicle?" Colton shielded his eyes and looked at the older model Ford coming down the lane.

Mark checked his phone calendar. "No. And I don't have anyone scheduled for a visit with one of the boys. Those have to be pre-approved and scheduled through their case manager."

"Well, let's just see what he wants." Colton offered Brandon one of the rockers on the porch. "We'll let you handle this, Mark."

Mark put his phone in his pocket and positioned himself on the top step, leaning against the post.

"Hello." The man stepped out of his car and flicked ashes from his cigarette on the ground.

Mark stepped down to the man and stretched out his hand. "Good afternoon. What can we do for you?"

The man failed to reciprocate, and Mark let his hand slide back down to his side.

"I'm here to get the boy. They told me he was here, and I could swing by and pick him up."

Colton watched boys come from several different directions and file into the back of the house, summoned for lunch.

"No one notified me." Mark frowned.

"Sorry about that. Short notice kind of thing. Go fetch him for me, we'll be on our way." The big man turned and eyed the straggling boys.

"What is your boy's name?"

The man flicked more ashes to the wind. "Billy, like as in Billy the Kid," he snickered.

"Let me call his case manager and confirm."

Colton stood up and moved to Mark's side.

"Well, that's not necessary. I already spoke to the sheriff, and he's the one who told me where my boy was."

"I doubt that," Brandon muttered.

"I'll still need to confirm. I work through his case manager. What was your name?"

"I guess I'll go get the sheriff then. I'll be back." The man climbed into his car and sped down the lane.

"Colton, can you and Brandon go lock up the gate? I'm going to call Billy's case manager." Mark brushed past Colton.

"Sure thing." Colton and Brandon loaded into Brandon's truck. "Mark, I know Billy saw that guy when he walked into the house. He was visibly shaken."

"I'll talk to him as soon as I'm off the phone

with the case manager."

After locking the gate, Colton slid back into the passenger seat. "If he does bring the sheriff, they'll both have to wait until we come and unlock it."

"A good plan."

Brandon and Colton stepped into the house, smelling lunch wafting in the air.

Mark had his phone up to his ear with the mouthpiece covered. "I'm on the phone with Ellie Jenkins, Billy's case manager, and she says his father signed away all parental rights a year ago."

"The gate's locked. I doubt he'll come back, but if he does, we'll call Ms. Jenkins and explain the situation." Colton looked up as the women came into the room. "Let's eat and enjoy this time together. If he comes back, we'll deal with it then."

"I'm all for that. I'm starving." Brandon agreed.

"Let's eat then." Mark spoke into the phone. "Ellie, I'll call you back if we have any trouble with the dad. Thanks for the information."

The adults ate in the dining room, and the boys took heaping plates out to the picnic tables. Potato salad, BBQ ribs, sweet tea, and rhubarb pie all were devoured. Colton watched out the window as Billy sat by himself, back up against the tree, casting wary glances at the house.

"Man, I need a nap." Brandon put his arm around the back of Selena's chair.

"We should probably go." Selena smacked him. "You don't want this oaf snoring on your couch."

"I don't know. The hammock on the back porch

is calling my name."

"I should probably go, too." Juliette stood and carried her empty plate to the kitchen.

"Mark, Mark." One of the younger boys collided with Juliette, worry etched on his face.

"What, Kyle? What's wrong?" Mark leaned down to his height.

"Billy's gone. I wanted him to play catch with me after lunch."

"Why do you think he's gone, Kyle?" Mark asked, glancing at Colton.

"He said he had to. But I didn't believe him. Now he's gone. Really, really gone."

"Kyle, maybe he didn't want to play catch right now."

"No, he ran away. Because of that man."

Mark looked at Colton. "Do you think he really did?"

Colton made a beeline to the bunkhouse, Mark close behind.

"All of his things are still here. Maybe he needed space after seeing his father here."

"Where would he go?" Colton eyed Billy's baseball mitt on top of his dresser.

"I don't know. Check the barn and make sure all of the horses are here. I'll go look at the perimeter cameras."

"Do you think he ran away?" Brynleigh bumped into Colton as she came into the bunkhouse.

"I have no idea. Hopefully, he just needed some time." Colton ran out to the barn. All of the horses were accounted for, even the tame one Billy always chose to ride.

He met Mark and the others in the front yard.

Colton shook his head at him, and Mark's face dropped.

"None of the cameras registered an alarm, so he has to still be on the property." Mark wiped his eyes.

"I've got one more place to look." Colton put up his hand. "Let me check first."

"Maybe we should pray?" Aunt Eunice put her hand on Mark's back and folded Brynleigh in on the other side. "Dear Heavenly Father, please locate Billy and show us how we can help him. Protect him as you've protected all of us. In Your Name. Amen."

Colton clenched and unclenched his hands as he walked towards the other side of the barn where the goats lived. Sweat rolled down his back. His aversion to the goats had lessened since his first encounter with them, but coupled with Billy missing and the boy's father showing up unexpectedly, well, triggers were starting to ignite. Breathe in 1, 2, 3, 4 and out.

Colton looked over the pens where they fed and watered the goats. In one corner, shadowed by a wooden trough, he saw Billy, legs crossed, holding the smallest goat. Oh boy. He pulled out his phone and texted Mark. *I found him. Give me a minute with him alone.* "Billy?"

The boy startled and then rearranged the baby goat on his lap. "What?"

"Kyle thought you had run away. We've been looking for you. Are you okay?"

Billy angrily looked at Colton.

Colton knew that look, knew it well. "Mind if I

sit?" He sat down on the dirty floor without waiting for Billy's response.

"Want to hold a goat, too?" Billy spat. "I can catch one for you."

"No, I'm good." Colton brushed off his taunt. "Why did Kyle think you'd run away?"

"Cuz' I told him I was going to."

"Why? Because of that man who stopped by?" Colton pushed hay around with his fingers.

Billy gave him a sidelong glance, "You know who that was, right?"

"I'm guessing your dad." The baby goat nudged Colton's arm. "But why tell Kyle you were going to run away? Did you see us make that guy leave? You're safe here."

"What if he wanted to tell me something about my mom? And you ran him off?"

Colton wracked his brain for anything he'd ever heard about Billy's mom. Nothing. Only what Ms. Jenkins had said about his dad. "He could have left a message with us, if that was the case. I don't think him being here had anything to do with your mom. You do know you're safe here, right?"

"Fat chance. In a couple of years, you won't even want to be around me. I'll be just like him. Why do you care anyway?"

"Well, I think you and I are a lot alike, and maybe we can help each other," Colton sighed, "plus, I've been learning a lot more about what is truth and what isn't."

"Dude, I don't even know what that means."

The baby goat stood up, stretched, and curled back down in Billy's lap, head facing Colton.

"Truth is whatever God says and God's saying-"

"Back to the God stuff? We've had this conversation before." Billy jumped to his feet, startling Colton and the goat. He sunk against the pen walls, back turned towards Colton. The goat circled his feet, bleating.

Colton could see the boy's shoulders shaking. Picking up the baby goat, he resisted the instinctual urge to put it back down. "Billy, look at me."

The boy turned his tear-stained face to Colton and eyed the goat in his arms.

"We can change. We don't have to be like our fathers." Colton stroked the baby goat's head, hand quivering slightly. "With God's help."

Colton was thrown off balance when Billy rushed headlong into him, wrapping skinny teenager arms around Colton's middle. The baby goat squeaked, squished between the two.

Colton let tears of his own flow down his face. Whatever it took with this kid, he wanted to be a part of showing him how much he was loved. Kindred wounded spirits.

You will know the truth and the truth will set you free.

NOT THE END

Have you ever felt like Brynleigh did, always having to earn someone's affection? Their loyalty? Their interest in you? If you didn't prove yourself to them, they would never like, much less love, you? Or maybe you've felt like Colton who made mistakes which, in his mind, equated to being worthless?

Genuine, life-altering feelings for both Brynleigh and Colton, and maybe you, too.

The father of lies, satan (or whatever you want to call him), your very real enemy wants you to take those feelings and act on them. The unforgiveness and shallow self-thoughts are products of a relationship built on conditional love. The enemy wants you to feel "less than" and "not enough" and uses our most basic desire, love, to encourage those feelings.

Colton battled failure like it was tattooed on his chest, written on his forehead, and impressed on his heart. His inability to stop his dad from physically abusing his mom because he was just a kid made him angry at himself, God, and anyone close to him. Fear of becoming like his dad created a vicious circle; Colton got angry and used his fists or self-medicated with whatever would numb the pain. Being medically discharged from a job he was good at because he was reckless only confirmed he was a worthless human being, unworthy of anything real.

The truth came to both Brynleigh and Colton as God intervened. Neither had role models of the faith until God brought Selena and Brandon into their lives, allowed them to see examples of truth, and whispered in their ears.

Although these are just characters in a book, I want you to know that God, in real life - your reality, is calling *your* name. Everyone has wounds and lies they've come to believe. Truth is God's opinion on any matter - including you. The enemy will always spin lies and tell you half-truths, but God, the one who created you, will always be truth.

These are His truths about you:

> 1)   He loves you unconditionally. You don't have to earn it, you don't have to be a certain way for Him to love you. You don't have to do certain things in exchange for love. He loves you.

> ***I pray that out of his glorious riches He may strengthen you with power through his Spirit in your inner being so that Christ may dwell in your hearts through faith. And I pray that you, being rooted and established in love, may have power, together with all the Lord's holy people, to grasp how wide and long and high and deep is the love of Christ, and to know this love that surpasses knowledge- that you may***

be filled to the measure of all the fullness of God. *Ephesians 3:16-19 (NIV)*

We will always honor and please the Lord, and your lives will produce every kind of good fruit. All the while, you will grow as you learn to know God better and better. We also pray that you will be strengthened with all his glorious power so you will have all the endurance and patience you need. May you be filled with joy, always thanking the Father. He has enabled you to share in the inheritance that belongs to his people, who live in the light. For he has rescued us from the kingdom of darkness and transferred us into the Kingdom of his dear Son, who purchased our freedom and forgave our sins. Colossians 1:9-14 (NLT)

2)   You were created for a purpose. If He didn't want you in this world for a reason, you wouldn't be here. His plan for your life was set in motion a long time ago. People make choices (sometimes bad ones) and have free will, but your life is worth more than you may ever know. And your failures? No one is

perfect, but your mistakes do not define you. Neither do people. Only God does.

Feelings lie. If the enemy can give you certain thoughts, he can encourage you to act on those thoughts. He wants you isolated, not knowing truth, and looking to everyone but God for validation.

God is truth and He is the only one who can set you free from shame, unforgiveness, anger, and bitterness. Let Him speak into your life and be free.

If you or someone you know is encountering
any form of abuse, please ask for help.
You do not deserve it. That's truth.
You are valuable. That's truth.
You are loved. That's truth.
Abuse Hotline 1-800-799-7233

If you or someone you know is struggling
with post traumatic stress,
there is help available for you, too. Do not be
ashamed or wait until it's controlling your life;
Proverbs 15:22 says, "Without counsel, plans fail.
With many advisors, they succeed."
Please ask for help.

Call or text 988 to speak to a trained crisis
counselor.
If you are a veteran, call 988 and press "1" to
talk to someone who has experience in military post
traumatic stress.

Other helplines available:
National Suicide Prevention Line- 800-273-
TALK (8255) 24/7
National Hopeline Network- 800-442-HOPE
(4673) 24/7
Substance Abuse and Mental Health Services
Administration- 800-662-HELP (4357) 24/7

Book Club discussion questions

1)What are some lies we believe about ourselves? About others?

2) Why do we believe those lies?

3) How do we find freedom from those lies?

4) Colton said to Brynleigh "It wasn't her actions or reactions that defined you." How do you define yourself? Who defines you?

5) Do you have people in your life that are toxic influences like Brynleigh's mother, Celeste? How do you balance them in your life?

6) We are often our worst enemy. What practical things can we do to minimize negative self-thinking?

7) What is love?

8) How do you know who God is and how He feels about you?

9) Why does knowing truth bring freedom?

Acknowledgements

Thank you, Heavenly Father, for creating me to tell stories, for giving me words and ideas and inspiration. This is Your good, good plan for my life and I am eternally grateful.

To the Reed men (Randy, Trevin, and Tyler)- thank you for sharing your heart, your experiences, and your insight into Colton. Randy, your wisdom in all matters is respected and I have always been inspired by your quiet strength. Trevin and Tyler- you both have made an impact on my family and your bravery and warrior personalities have, and will continue, to touch many lives. It doesn't hurt to have a strong, supportive, and prayerful momma like you do. I love your family!

To Cora- thank you for all of the brainstorming, critiquing, toes-in-the-sand conversations. Your encouragement and prayers are always a Godsend to me.

To Peggy- thank you for going on this journey with me. Your insightful questions and thoughts helped shape this book. (Who knew real farm wives don't wash their eggs before refrigerating them?!)

To Cynthia- thank you for your support and guidance. I know I drive you crazy with my questions, need for advice in the wee hours of the morning, and random thoughts. I would not be on this journey if it wasn't for you.

Other Books by Julie Brown

<u>Truth=Freedom Series</u> (a romantic suspense series)
Chained to a Dream- Book 1

<u>EVEN WHEN Series</u> (an inspirational non-fiction series on grief and loss)
God's Promises are Still True EVEN WHEN
God's Promises are Still True EVEN WHEN Companion Workbook

I love comments and feedback from readers!

Want to chat? Visit me at www.juliebrown-author.com or julie@juliebrown-author.com. I'd love to hear from you!

Julie Brown has a degree in Criminal Justice and has worked with juvenile offenders, teens in crisis, and in a penitentiary. She became a widow in 2021 and has firsthand knowledge of how grief and loss can be an all-consuming, hard journey. Through that experience, she published an inspirational non-fiction series titled God's Promises are Still True EVEN WHEN. Julie writes from her back porch in Missouri where the hummingbirds fly, the coffee is sweet, and friends are welcomed.

www.ingramcontent.com/pod-product-compliance
Lightning Source LLC
Chambersburg PA
CBHW061149210726
48294CB00006B/1635